ROYAL
CHAOS

ALSO BY LARAMIE BRISCOE

The Haldonia Monarchy

Royal Rebel

ROYAL CHAOS

A Haldonia Monarchy Novel

LARAMIE BRISCOE

ROYAL CHAOS

CHAPTER 1
AMELIA

"How is marriage treating you?"

I smile gently as I glance at the female reporter sitting across from me. It's the most popular question I get asked. Since our wedding, it's what everyone wants to know.

To be honest, it's my favorite thing to talk about. I don't mind answering.

"Very well." I clasp my hands in my lap, allowing my wedding ring to show. A move perfected in the seven weeks since I became a wife. "It's been the best decision I've ever made."

"But was it really *yours*?"

She's brave. The first reporter to broach the circumstances surrounding our marriage. I've been coached on how to answer, but it's hard not to allow my irritation to show.

"Yes, it *was* my decision. From a very young age, I knew my destiny, the expectation of what my life would entail. Was I nervous at first? Of course, but Tristan is the *best* person I've ever met."

"I'm sure others would say differently."

"I'm sure others don't know him the way I do." I tilt my chin at her. "They don't see us in private moments or how he treats me as the woman in his life. While we may not have had what many would call a traditional courtship, it's a love story nonetheless."

"You're a better woman than I, Queen Amelia."

My eyes meet Shannon's across the room. I nod almost imperceptibly. We've become perfectionists at it.

"I'm sorry to interrupt." She comes into view of the reporter. "But the queen has another appointment. If you'd like to book a follow-up interview, please contact our office."

She stands, holding her hand out to me. Most people in my presence would curtsy, but something tells me she won't give me the satisfaction. Instead of putting her in her place, I shake her hand.

"Thank you for taking the time to speak with me."

"My pleasure." I give her the smile I'm supposed to and watch as she's escorted out.

When the door shuts, I plop into the chair, sighing heavily. Sometimes having to be polite in the face of rudeness is the worst part of what I have to do.

Shannon comes back into the room, giving me a look as she has a seat across from me. "She was interesting."

"She was a bitch," I mumble.

"Amelia." She laughs.

"She was," I defend myself. "Just because I'm not supposed to say it doesn't mean I won't."

"Which is why I love working with you."

"Thank God. If you didn't enjoy working with me, I'm not sure what I would do."

"You'd find someone else."

I glance over at her. "Not sure anyone else could put up with me."

"Oh, I'm positive someone else would put up with you."

Sighing, I lean forward, taking some of the strain off my back from sitting properly. "What's next on my agenda?"

The door opens, and I'm met with the man who makes my heart beat a little faster each time I see him. "How about lunch with me?"

"What are you doing here?" I jump up from my chair, launching myself into his arms.

We saw each other last night at dinner, but you'd have no idea given the way I greet him. This morning, he was gone when I woke up, and I wasn't able to start my day off the way I'm used to.

"We got done early," he explains. "I had Parker swing by the pub you like. Got you a pint and some lunch. Sound good?"

King of Haldonia, and he's still willing to take time out of his busy day to do the little things that make me happy. "Sounds great."

He turns, clearing his throat. "Parker, Shannon. Do you mind?"

They glance at each other, smiles toying with the edges of their lips. "I think I know what you're saying." Parker chuckles. "We'll be available if you need us."

Tristan doesn't waste a glance at them. "I'm sure the two of us will do just fine."

"Duly noted." Parker opens the door, holding it for Shannon.

"Never thought they'd leave," I whisper, standing up on tiptoe to fuse my lips with his. Before they meet, he pulls back slightly.

"Sometimes they need a little push."

Tilting my head to the side, I lean forward to where they're almost touching. "Looks like you need a little push too."

One of his arms slips from around my waist, his fingers tangling in my hair. "Are you having pictures made this afternoon?"

"Nope." I shake my head, my eyes fluttering downward to his mouth. "You can mess me up as much as you like. The rest of my day I'll be sitting behind this desk going through our correspondence. No more interviews." I wrinkle my nose.

"Was your interview bad earlier?"

"Nothing a kiss won't fix." I lick my lips in anticipation, hoping he'll give me everything I want.

His gaze moves down before he grips my hair tight, pulling my body into his space. We meld, fusing ourselves together. My fingers grab hold of the dress shirt covering his torso. What I wouldn't give to have a few hours alone with him in the middle of the day, where he wasn't needed by someone, and I had nothing to do. The only days we're allowed to truly be ourselves are the weekends we spend at the beach.

Those strong fingers of his caress my ass, gripping tightly. His lips let go, smearing along my neck, nipping at the column of my throat.

I'm drunk on the kiss, inebriated on him, and everything he does to me.

In front of the world, he's all buttoned up and proper.

With me? He's everything I've always wanted in my own love story. The strength to my weaknesses, the bold to my shy, the understanding to my anxiety. Tristan lifts me up and holds me tight, never letting me fall against the pressures of what we're trying to do for our country.

Pulling apart, we rest our foreheads together. He breathes deeply.

"I guess we should get this lunch on the road. Parker will show up expecting me to be ready for my afternoon, and all I'll be doing is walking around with a hard-on and an empty stomach."

I giggle, pressing against his chest. "If the people only knew the way you talk to me in private."

"If the people only knew the way you take me down your throat." He grasps my chin with his thumb and forefinger, tilting my face up to his. "But that's just between us, isn't it, Lia?"

I bite my bottom lip, grabbing hold of his shirt collar. "Our little secret. Come on, let's get to lunch."

We have a seat on the couch in the back of my office, where I start setting out the food and beer he brought for us.

"Do I get bonus points for bringing you a pint?" he teases, raising his eyebrow as he grasps his glass, pulling it toward his lips.

Diving in, I grab hold of the pint, stealing the drink, moaning as it slides down my throat. "That's good stuff." I smack my lips together. "And you do get bonus points for bringing me my own, but yours always tastes better."

He shakes his head, an astonished grin on his face. "You're lucky I love you."

"I know." I wrinkle my nose up at him.

Instead of arguing, I start to lay out our Styrofoam containers, my mouth watering as I smell the fish and chips. It's the freshest in town, not as good as what's up north by the beach, but it's tasty enough that I want it at least a few times a week.

"They tried to give it to me." He grabs a piece of fish. "Instead of paying for it. They wanted to gift it to someone who could purchase it a million times over. Apparently my father was a regular, and he never paid for his meals there."

"Does that make you angry?" I take a bite, chewing thoughtfully.

"I want our country to succeed." He stops for a second. "It doesn't seem right. I would use my position of power in a way that doesn't set us up to do so."

I'm proud of him, possibly prouder than I've ever been. "You're a good man, Tristan, and an even better king."

He smiles, taking a drink from his pint glass. "As long as I can improve on the one before me, that's all I care about."

Leaning over at the man I call my husband, I wrap my arms around his waist. "Haldonia's lucky to have you."

He drops his lips to my forehead. "And I you."

There's a feeling I have about him. He'll be the leader written in the history books, and I want nothing more than to stand by his side. None of it will be easy, but together, I know we can do anything we set our minds to.

CHAPTER 2
TRISTAN

"What else do I have going on?"

Parker looks at me, a sardonic eyebrow raised. "Sir, I'm your protection detail, not your secretary."

I point to the phone that's on speaker, giving him back as good as I got. "I wasn't asking you."

"He was asking *me*." The voice of the woman who keeps my life together comes over the line. Kate is new, but damned if she's not the best assistant I've ever had.

"Yeah, I was talking to Kate. What else do I have going on?" I ask again, daring Parker to interrupt this time.

"The rest of your week appears to be on the light side. No appearances, a few interviews."

This news gives me hope. "Maybe Amelia and I can get out of here early on Friday? We're heading up to the beach house." Which is what I want more than anything. Time alone with her has become my favorite way to spend a few hours, and I'll do whatever it takes to make it a priority.

She's flipping through papers if the sound coming over the line is any indication. "You can leave early in the morning if you really want to."

This is music to my ears. If there's anything we need to keep our sanity, it's our weekends away. Although we've been able to spend all of them since we got married at the beach house, there're some times when we need it more than others. This is one of them.

"Let's plan on it." I point to Parker, making sure he's good to go. "Eleven on Friday?"

He nods, which is all I need to verify we're leaving the city.

"Should be doable," she answers. "Make sure you get what has to be done, completed, and I'll be okay with it."

"Shoot." I grab my pen. "Tell me exactly what you're expecting."

She starts in with an itemization of tasks as I scribble furiously, trying to keep up. I find a handwritten list is more tangible to me rather than an electronic one. "The most important is to make sure the interviews are done before you leave. If you want me to, I can move them up and have it all completed in one day."

"That sounds amazing." I stop writing, thinking of what I can do with the extra time. "Can you please get with Shannon and make sure she knows I'm trying to get us out of here early on Friday?"

"Okay, give me a couple of hours, and I'll report back with what I've got for you. I'll also loop Shannon in."

We end the phone call, and I turn to look at Parker. There's a conversation I've wanted to have with him. Now seems like the perfect time. "Did you find anything at the beach house or on the security footage?"

He shakes his head. "I know you said you felt like someone was watching you, but there's nothing I've found." He rubs at his beard. "Could it be that you're slightly paranoid now that you have a monarchy and a wife?"

"I'm many things." I rub my hand over my forehead, hoping to dull the pain gathering behind my eyes. "Paranoid isn't one of them."

"Are you sure? My king, there honestly wasn't anything I saw."

Something about this doesn't sit right with me, but if Parker says he hasn't seen a threat, then I have to believe him. He's the one person in my life who never lied to me. "We'll keep an eye out, won't we?"

He tilts his head to the side. "When do I not make sure you're protected, sir?"

I have to hand it to him, I *am* constantly safe. I can count on two fingers the number of times I've been worried when Parker was in charge of my care. Both instances were freak accidents, not something I would ever blame him for. "Never," I admit. "But I have more than myself to think about now."

"You and the queen are my top priority."

"If it comes down to it, I want you to take care of her and not me."

"No can do, sir, and you know that. You have to be the one I'm worried about. You run this country."

"But without her, it won't matter," I argue, feeling the despair in the pit of my stomach.

"It has to. If anyone, friend or foe, sees she means that much to you, they'll target her."

What he says is true, but how does one turn off love and adoration? "How am I supposed to hide it?"

This is the part I find difficult. Prior to Amelia, there wasn't anyone who had me, not like her, and now the thought of losing her, of not being as happy as we are in this moment, is enough to send me into a tailspin.

"I think you'll figure it out." Parker has a seat in the chair in front of my desk. "In my experience, when we have someone to fight for, it comes naturally."

"Nothing like this has ever been natural for me. You know how my parents were."

"The way you were brought up doesn't have to define what your future holds."

"Huh," I grunt. "Easy for you to say."

"It honestly isn't, but when I look at the two of you, I see a bond so strong I'm not sure anyone or anything will ever be able to break it. What you have is special, and I know asking you to dial it back in public isn't what you want to hear."

"If I do it too much, will there be an issue with that?"

He shrugs. "The public will do whatever it is they want. They'll believe what the media feeds to them, or they'll see what's in front of their own two eyes."

"I hope you're right."

"I always am."

I throw a pen at him, which the fucker catches one-handed. As much as I appreciate him being number one at his job, sometimes I'd like to best him. "Yeah, yeah." I shake my head. "Let me get busy."

He laughs. "I'll be outside if you need me."

I watch as he leaves. This is one of the only times a day I'm alone. After lunch, figuring out the last half of my day. It's the few hours I can truly be myself. Reaching up, I loosen my tie, unbuttoning the two buttons at my throat and making room to breathe. Standing up, I take off my coat, rolling up the sleeves to my elbows, before sitting down and pulling the papers on my desk directly in front of me.

There's not a lot here, a few issues that have become extremely important to me since I became king, but most of this is tedious and time-consuming. Parker and my adviser tell me I should hire someone to take care of things like this, but it almost makes me feel as if I'm not doing my job.

My father did a lot of his leading in name only. Me? I want to do mine from the front. If there's anything I've learned, it's how *not* to lead, and my legacy will be much different than the one before me. Even if it was a huge point of contention with dear old dad.

"Tristan, you have to prove to your people that you won't bend."

"I don't agree. Sometimes you have to so that the country doesn't break. There's not a one size fits all manual for leading."

"Yes, there is," he argues. "I've given you the best economic platform to stand on in decades, and you're going to run it into the ground."

"The top one percent of our people has food on the table. The other ninety-nine? They're doing their best to have a table to put food on," I yell, wanting him to see things from my perspective.

"The top one percent is what makes this country thrive."

"No, it doesn't. They don't do the hard work that no one else wants to do. They hold the purse strings, but without the workers, where would we be?"

I'm breathing hard, wishing he would see the truth.

"If there's no money, then there's nothing to run the country with, Tristan."

"Dad, if there are no workers, then who runs the country?" I counter.

He doesn't say anything, just shakes his head as he crosses his arms over his chest. "We're not going to be able to come to an agreement about this."

"You're right, we won't," I agree. "There's no way you won't convince me the richest of this country are the most important."

Sighing, I lean forward, grabbing my pen, getting to work. Thinking about my dad will get me nowhere. Instead I need to focus on what I can change, not my past. My past is what got me here. My future is what will keep me where I am.

For this country, for Lia, for any children we might have, the future needs to be bright. It has to be.

I won't allow it to be anything but.

CHAPTER 3
AMELIA

"How do you want your hair tonight?"

Glancing up, I see the stylist who normally works with me standing over my head, running her fingers through the length. Our eyes lock in the mirror before I shiver.

"It's slightly cold." I look out at the nighttime sky. It's not yet summer but still has the chill of spring barely turning from winter. The frigid temps are hanging around this year. "Let's go with down."

Meghan nods, and I already see the wheels turning in her mind. "Sounds good. Do you want curls?"

"Always." I grin, knowing it's Tristan's favorite way for me to wear it.

"Celeste is here." Shannon comes sweeping into the room with the makeup artist I've grown to love.

It's taken both Tristan and me a while to become comfortable with our own decisions, but we're getting there. The first thing we did once we took office was let go of most of his father's staff. They didn't have the same beliefs we do, and in order for Haldonia to prosper, we all have to be united. We each have our favorite people to work with and an excellent support system around us.

"Hey." I give her a wave, along with a warm grin.

"Hey." She smiles in return. "Sorry I'm late, it was hard to get through security."

Meghan makes a noise in her throat. "It was. First time I've ever had an issue. Is something going on we need to know about?"

This is the first I'm hearing of it, and I make a note to ask Tristan or Parker later. "Not that I'm aware of, but I'll keep you informed if there is."

"How do you want your makeup tonight, my queen?"

We all snicker, still not used to my title. With them I can be myself and not have to put on any kind of pretenses. They've all become close to me, and for that, I'm thankful. "I'm wearing the gray dress over there." I point to an off-the-shoulder number with lace and crystals. The train is long and flowing, much different than anything I've ever worn before.

"We can do ultra-feminine or dark and smoky. Your choice."

"Let's do ultra-feminine. I haven't gone that route in a while."

Celeste nods before she gets to work. "Wednesday night is an interesting one to have a get-together like this."

"Agreed, but I found out earlier today, because of this, Tristan and I can head up the coast on Friday." I sigh, thinking about the time we'll get to spend together.

"Listen to her sigh," Meghan laughs. "Don't we all wish we had the kind of love story they have?"

"It hasn't always been perfect," I argue, not wanting anyone to think we haven't fought for what we have.

"Sure, it hasn't," both of them say together.

"We didn't even know each other before his birthday. That was the first day we ever met," I remind them, thinking back to that night. I'd been so nervous, but the kiss we shared still lives on in my memory. "Granted, we had time to get to know one another afterward, but I'm still learning new things about him every single day."

"That's kinda fun though, right?" Meghan picks up the curling iron and quickly winds a lock of hair around it. "Half the fun of dating is gaining knowledge about the other person. It's gotta be magnified when you're married. I imagine the two of you sorta play twenty questions in a sexual way."

"Oh my god." I laugh, putting my hand over my mouth. "I love when we all get together. It reminds me of being with my friends at university."

"Yet she hasn't answered the question." Celeste's look is cheeky, her eyes bright with her teasing tone. "They're probably playing all kinds of games, so to speak."

My face burns, but at the same time, I enjoy being with all of them. This is the space I get to be the young woman I am. Giggling about my husband, talking about our new marriage, and learning what it means to be in charge of my sexuality. "Maybe we are." I shrug.

Shannon snorts from where she sits. "They most definitely are."

"And you and Parker would know better than anyone." Celeste looks over my shoulder to wink at Shannon. "Speaking of Parker, must be nice to be in his presence all the time. Mr. Tall, Dark, and Handsome."

It's Shannon's turn to blush, and I revel in it.

"Yeah." I lock eyes with her through the mirror, teasing her the same way she did to me. "What does it mean to be around him all the time? Huh?"

She throws a piece of paper at all of us. "It's not like that. He and I are put together so much because of our jobs."

"Mmm hmmm." I reach over, taking a drink of the water beside me. "You keep telling yourself that."

"So, when do Meghan and I get our own detail? I mean, we're not expendable. We know how to do your hair and makeup like no one else. Does Parker have brothers?"

"A younger one," Shannon mumbles as she continues looking at the laptop in front of her.

Celeste and Meghan stop what they're doing to turn and look at her. "Yeah...you don't care at all," Meghan snorts before she turns back around, continuing to work on my hair.

Shannon laughs as she winks at Meghan. "It'll have to be our little secret."

I keep it to myself, but I'm woman enough to admit Parker is definitely something else, and I'm lucky I get to see him all the time with my husband.

"So, what are you and Tristan doing tonight? Where are you going?" Celeste asks as she continues working on my makeup. "I think I heard something about it being for children."

"Yes! I'm excited. It's an initiative to get kids to stay in school and to get help for food stability. It's something important to both myself and Tristan," I explain. "Neither one of us has had to deal with insta- bility like either one of those things, and our hope is no child in Haldonia will ever have to deal with it again."

Meghan makes a noise in the back of her throat. "It sounds like a good idea. I'm one of those kids who grew up without food stability, and I really wish someone had been worried about me. The sad truth is no one ever knew about it, because I was too embarrassed to admit it."

"That's our goal." I smile at her in the mirror. "It's one of the talking points we feel is most important to making sure Haldonia has a fighting chance in the next century. Our kids need to be able to compete on the global stage. For us, the future is way more influen- tial than the past. It's going to be hard to correct the mistakes that Tristan's father made, but we are trying to do what we think is right."

Shannon smiles from where she sits behind us. "And I'm beyond proud to be a part of it."

"Okay," Celeste says. "I think you're done, and you're definitely going to knock everyone's socks off."

When she moves back from the mirror my eyes widen in surprise as I see what I look like. Sometimes I think I will never be prettier than I was the day I married Tristan, but these ladies keep making me look like a supermodel every single time. "Are you sure this is me?" I reach up to touch my hair.

Meghan giggles. "Yes, this is you. We work with what we have, and you're one of the best canvases we're blessed to work on."

"Thank you both! I need to get dressed now, but I can't tell you how much I appreciate you always coming through whenever I ask you for your help."

"It's truly my pleasure, Queen." Celeste snickers one last time.

Shannon stands up, motioning me with her hands. She's looking down at her cell phone and beginning to slightly panic. "We have to get you ready within the next twenty minutes. Tristan and Parker will be here to pick us both up."

"I guess that means I'll be seeing you all later. Be sure and look for me on the front pages of all the magazines tomorrow."

"I'm sure you will be, Queen." Meghan begins packing up her hair tools while Celeste does the same with her makeup.

"It doesn't mean I'm not nervous. I always am."

"Well, you look like a million bucks no matter what." Celeste bows slightly to me.

"Thanks to you." I curtsy back to her.

"Are you comfortable with the way this fits? It shows a little much for you," Shannon asks as she helps me into my dress.

"Yeah, I know." I'm looking over my shoulder in the mirror. "I'm always slightly self-conscious, but it is what it is."

"There is no reason for you to be worried. Both of us know that."

"It's easy for you to say. You're not on the cover of every magazine and newspaper the next morning after some huge event. It never fails. I see all my flaws as soon as the first one is released."

"True, but if my husband looked at me the way yours looks at you? I wouldn't worry at all."

My cheeks turn red as I think about the man she's speaking of. He does look at me as if I'm the only person in the world. It's one of the things I enjoy most about our relationship. There's a knock at the door. One I've heard before. It's the strong rasp of my husband's knuckles.

"Are you decent?" he asks before coming in.

"You didn't wait to see if I was going to answer." I laugh as I give him a look from the top of his head to the bottom of his feet. He wears a tuxedo like nobody's business. His dark hair falls slightly over the side of his right eye, giving him a hint of boyishness and just enough of the badass he is.

There aren't many people who can rule a country the way he does. I know for a fact it keeps him up late at night. Sometimes when I wake up to roll over or to get a drink of water, he's standing at the window observing his kingdom. No doubt worrying whether he's doing the right thing or not. Honestly, I wouldn't have it any other way.

"Are you ready to go get this show on the road?"

"Definitely, and did I hear you right that we get to leave early for the beach?"

"Yes." He leans down, grabbing my hand with his, bringing it up to his lips. It's a chaste kiss on the back of my palm, one of the small touches I cherish. "We do get to leave early, which means we get a long weekend."

One of the first four-day lounge-fests we've had since we got married. "Will you have to do any work while we're there?" I ask, an eyebrow raised. Sometimes he tells me we get time together, but he's stuck behind his desk with his laptop open and his brain hard at work thinking up ways to fix messed-up policies.

"No." He pulls me into his hard chest. "There will be no work on this trip. It'll just be you and me."

"That's exactly what I wanted to hear. I'll hold you to that, Tris."

"Please do." He bends over at the waist, dipping low in front of me.

"Shouldn't I be the one bowing to you?"

He looks around to see if anyone's listening. But Parker and Shannon are too busy whispering to one another. He lightly grips the back of my neck pulling me even closer to his lips. I can feel his hot breath against my skin when he whispers. "The only way I want you bowing is over the back of the bed or my desk."

My cheeks heat as I think about what he says.

Before I can reply, Parker is speaking again. "Sir, are we ready to go?"

"Lia?" Tristan asks, a shit-eating grin on his face.

"As ready as you are." I avert my eyes from him like the proper lady I am.

"Then let's go, everyone."

Tristan leads us out, me by his side where I know I'll spend every day until the day I die.

CHAPTER 4
TRISTAN

One of my least favorite parts of being in the public eye is having to do events like these. While they are important, I often feel as if they take away from the magnitude of what my constituents and I are trying to do. Everyone gets caught up in the pomp and circumstance, all the glamour. Unless faced with it every day, they seem to forget there's a percentage of Haldonia who can't put food on the table or a roof over their head.

At that same time, I have to admit—I'm still a red-blooded man. The best part about these events is seeing Lia dressed up the way she is. Since our marriage was arranged, and we spent most of our time at the beach house, I never got to see her dress up for a date and surprise me like other couples do.

There's been a few nights similar to this one, where we've gotten dressed separately, seeing each other for the first time when we're wearing our adult clothes and me being surprised by how beautiful she is.

These nights out are the equivalent of those dates. The ones where we knew nothing about each other and learned to get along while having our disagreements.

We sit in the back of a chauffeured bulletproof Range Rover, Parker driving directly behind us. All around, standing on the sidewalks and lining the streets, are large groups of citizens, watching and waving as we make our way to the hotel hosting our event tonight. Reaching over, I grab her hand in mine, rubbing against the back of her palm. "You look amazing," I whisper for her ears only.

"Don't look bad yourself there, King." She grins.

Something about the way she says my title gets to me. The sides of my mouth tilt in a sardonic smirk. "I can be your king later."

She giggles, hiding her mouth behind her hand in case someone is to take a picture and wonder what we're talking about. Yet another invasion of privacy we've both had to get used to. Not only paparazzi, but average citizens taking pictures of private moments, thinking they're invited into our world.

It's been hard to set boundaries, almost impossible really, but we have to if we want to make our marriage work.

"How long do we have to be here tonight?" she asks, leaning into my body.

I sigh, tilting my head back against the seat, tired from the day I've already had. Honestly, not looking forward to having to schmooze for the rest of the night. "Hopefully no more than a few hours."

She groans. "That means it's going to be at least three."

Slinging my arm around her neck, I pull her in closer. "We gotta do what we gotta do, babe."

"Can I give you a sign when I'm ready to go?"

A chuckle works its way out of my throat. "You can, but that doesn't mean I'll be able to accommodate you."

She turns half sideways in her seat, causing me to move my arm from around her shoulders.

Her fingers clench about my bicep, leaning into my neck and dropping a small kiss against the flesh. "I can't wait until this weekend," she whispers. "I cherish our time up north, and it's nice to have it alone."

"That we do," I agree with her. Privacy has been hard to come by lately, especially with us trying to get our initiatives set up. The inquisitiveness about our marriage is overwhelming. The number of interview requests has been daunting, not only for me but for her as well. "Speaking of, how did your interview go today?"

She snorts, pulling at a piece of lint on her skirt. "Something tells me you may have slept with that interviewer before. Because she asked me if the arranged marriage was my decision, and then I told her you're one of the best men I've ever met, and she said others may disagree."

I adjust in my seat hoping to not show how uncomfortable this makes me. There were a lot of things I did before I met Amelia. Dated women I shouldn't have, left them in the middle of the night without an explanation, but all of that was me trying to come to grips with who I was. The truth is, I didn't know until I met Amelia. She gave me that sense of purpose no other woman ever gave me. "What was her name?"

Amelia looks as if she doesn't want to tell me, like she's afraid I had a relationship with her at one time whether it be one night or longer.

"Philippa Becker," she answers, naming one of the most popular journalists in Haldonia. She's the head writer of one of the biggest gossip rags.

"Why did you even take an interview with her?"

"Shannon set it up," she defends herself. "We do our best to say yes to everyone who applies. None of us want to be accused of playing favorites. That's one of the biggest issues we face," she explains like I don't understand what she deals with.

"Still, you shouldn't have given her the time of day."

"Because of what she writes or because of who she is to you, Tristan?"

Her voice is annoyed, and this is definitely not how I want this night to go, but sometimes you have to have the hard discussions

"I do know her," I confirm. "She and I had a relationship."

"A relationship or a one-night stand?" she retorts.

"It was a relationship," I groan. "One of the few I ever had before we met."

"Why didn't you tell me? That way I could have avoided the embarrassment."

Now I'm growing irritated, and I do my best to keep my voice level. "Do I have to tell you about every relationship I had before we met? You haven't told me about every relationship you had."

"It's not like there were many, Tristan. I wasn't allowed to be like you."

This pisses me off. I grind my back teeth together before I look at my wife. "Nobody ever said I was perfect, and I never claimed to be."

"This isn't about you being perfect, Tristan. This is about you giving me a heads up."

"How am I supposed to give you a heads up if I don't know who you're meeting with?"

"Well, should I start clearing everything with you from now on? That way I know if I'm walking into something that's bound to embarrass me." She crosses her arms over her chest, running her hands up and down her bare shoulders. "Now I dread the article she's going to write. I told her no one knows you like I do."

My voice is soft as I explain. "No one does. You're the only person who's ever taken the time to get to know the real me. Everyone else wanted to know who was going to be the next king. But you, you wanted to know who Tristan was."

"So I'm supposed to feel sorry for you because you didn't let people in? Tristan, that was as much your damage as anyone else's."

"That's not what I'm saying at all. What I'm trying to explain is she didn't care about who I was as a person. All she wanted was the title."

"Can we not do this right now? I don't want people to see us upset with one another."

"I didn't want to do this to begin with," I remind her. "You're the one who asked the questions. I have a past I can't change. All I care about is the future." My voice is getting slightly louder, but it's because I want her to understand exactly what I'm saying. "I made mistakes, and there's nothing I can do about them. I can't change it now, and I don't want to. The past brought me to you." I finish up much softer than I started.

"But sometimes it feels like your past is way more important than our present."

"My present is everything I've always wanted, Amelia. Everything. It took me a while to get here, but only because of the way I grew up.

I'm all in with you right now. I don't want you to think differently. You are the most important part of my life."

The driver turns. "We're almost there, sir."

She makes a noise. "Which means we have to act like things are okay, even when they aren't."

"I want us to be good, not to be angry with one another. This is stupid, Amelia. I care about you more than I've ever cared about anyone else. You are my future in my present."

"I know," she says once and then again. "I know. It's hard realizing you had a life before me, and I have to see it. You don't have to see mine. There was only one other person." She takes a deep breath, seeming to pull herself together.

"If I could go back and change it, I would. Please believe me. The only thing I can do is move forward." I reach over and grab her chin between my thumb and forefinger, forcing her to meet my gaze. "I love you. You know it's not easy for me to say, but I tell you every day, because I want you to know. I need you to know it."

As we pull up, there's a red carpet, and cameras are already flashing. I feel her change before me just as I changed before her. Gone is the annoyance with one another, and in its place are the masks we wear in public so that we're not front page news with grumpy faces. The last thing we need are stories saying we're not happy. It's hard enough to be newlyweds, even harder when people make assumptions about whether we'll make it or not.

"You don't have to worry. No one will know we're arguing." She grabs hold of my hand.

"It shouldn't be an argument," I whisper in her ear. "I love you. Even if I wasn't King of Haldonia, even if this wasn't an arranged marriage, I think we would have met one another. I believe we were meant to be together, and I need you to believe that too."

She smiles sweetly. "I do."

As we step out onto the red carpet, we turn to wave to the people who have been captivated by our love story. And as we hold hands walking toward the front door, I know the two of us are supposed to be, and for once, I thank my father. This is the one thing he actually did right.

CHAPTER 5
AMELIA

Flashbulbs go off from each and every direction as we make another stop on the red carpet, turning to face the throng of reporters. This is where I feel the most out of my element. It's never been the place where I'm comfortable, nor do I necessarily enjoy it. I do realize at some point I'll have to get used to it because this is my life now, and I've signed up for the long haul. Tristan squeezes my hand as we greet everyone who's gathered to see us tonight. People and cameras go as far as my eyes can see.

Tristan entwines his fingers with mine, his voice soft so that only I can hear. "Smile for me, Lia."

Even if I didn't feel like it at this moment, I'd do it for him because of the lilt of his voice. It's got a boyish innocence to it. One I don't hear often. At the same time, I have slight anxiety because I know if we don't seem happy with one another, it will be the first thing on the front pages tomorrow morning. Looking over at my husband, I give the biggest smile, because I am happy we're together and on the red carpet. No matter if we've just had a little tiff, this is still my favorite place to be.

Looking out among the crowd, I see a group of small children. They're holding out a couple of bouquets. Glancing over at Parker and the detail he has for the night I nod to the group, asking quickly. "Is it okay for me to go get that?"

He glances over to where I've indicated. "Yes. Let me make sure someone goes with you."

I lie back for a few moments until I see a member of the security detail walking toward me. Letting go of Tristan's hand, I quickly make my way over to them.

The kids run to me, all smiling as they see me bending down. The littlest one grins the biggest. "You are the cutest thing I've ever seen." I grab the flowers they are holding out to me.

"Queen Amelia!" Their voices are full of excitement. "We brought this for you!"

"Thank you so much! This is my favorite thing all night," I tell them as I hold the flowers tightly in my fingers. "Are your parents letting you stay up late?"

"Yes, they're keeping us home from school tomorrow since we're up past our bedtimes tonight."

A memory of my mom letting me do the same thing when we would come to events like this, to meet the king and queen, plays back in my head. I only met her once, and it was as if she was larger than life. All the glitter on her dresses and the sparkling of the diamonds. The bright colors of the jewels and her crown, the rings on her hands. The dark, rich hues of her dress. It was some of the most magical memories I've ever had. Once I learned who I would be and what my destiny was, I thought about the colors of the jewels and dresses I would wear, and I would wonder if I would appear to be as beautiful as she was. I can only hope that I am half the person she was.

Tristan comes over, gently grabbing my elbow, letting me know that it's time for us to leave. Parker is already standing at the entrance waiting for us. I glance back down at the children, sorry that I have to leave. "You all be good for your parents now, and thank you so much for the flowers."

They smile brightly, promising to do what their mother asks before Tristan and I make our way inside the ballroom. I feel the gazes on me as we enter.

This is still something I'm not used to, being the center of attention, people wondering what dress I'm wearing, what jewels I have on. Who did my hair and makeup? Wanting to have a duplicate of all my clothing. I can feel them looking me up and down, judging how I appear, more than likely seeing the doubt in my eyes. The doubt is something I haven't been able to overcome. Instead of it not bothering me as much as it did in the beginning, it's started to bother me more. I haven't told Tristan about it, or anyone else for that matter.

It's my little secret.

Or not so little.

"Are you ready?" he asks as he escorts me to our table.

Neither one of us has to give a speech tonight, which is a blessing. We can enjoy the night out and be ourselves.

When we're seated, I don't recognize the people sitting with us, but Tristan seems to. He goes around the table introducing me to members of the cabinet that vote on the issues for Haldonia. I do my best to keep their names in my mind, but I know I'll never remember them all.

He leans into my ear, whispering softly. I can feel the breath move the hair, and it causes a shiver to work its way down my back. "Don't worry, Lia. You won't have to say a word to these people. They're just happy to sit at the same table with you."

"And I'm just happy to sit with you," I answer, an impish smirk on my face.

He chuckles darkly. "Words can't express how badly I wish tonight was just the two of us."

I've had that same wish lately. Everything has been pushed onto us. Appearances here, appearances there. No time together and trying to make everything work. It's hard, especially when you're newlyweds. Harder when the eyes of a nation are upon you. Instead of telling him I understand, I lean into his arm. "Don't worry. It'll be just the two of us soon."

He's about to say something else when someone takes the podium at the front of the room. I settle in, ready for a night of long speeches. Trying to pretend like I'm interested when really all I can think about is the man sitting next to me and when exactly we can leave for the beach.

It feels like hours until the speeches come to an end and dinner is put in front of us. Small talk is the name of the game as I try to keep up with everything everyone says to my husband. Sometimes I wonder how he does it all, how he knows what to say and when to say it. How to schmooze and when to leave it alone.

It's so much to remember. Such a fine line to walk. One wrong word and you've pissed off a nation. A right one and you've made them happy for years to come. It's pressure, pressure that I don't know either one of us was prepared to deal with.

When there's a lag in conversation, I signal to Parker that I need to go to the women's restroom. He responds back that he understands what I'm asking for. There's a woman standing next to him who I'm sure is my detail for the night. She comes over, pulling my chair out. It's then that Tristan notices I'm ready to get up.

"Do you need help?" he asks.

"No," I answer, shaking my head. "Just a trip to the ladies' room. I have my shadow, and I'll be back in a moment."

He nods, his eyes looking anxious, which is odd. I'm protected, and there's no reason for him to be uneasy. Again, it reminds me to ask him later if something is going on.

He drops a kiss to the back of my hand. "Please be careful."

"Always." I give it a squeeze.

My detail and I—I've learned not to ask anything about them. I have a different one each time I go to the women's restroom. Another thing I've learned is to wait until they tell me it's okay to proceed. She looks under all the stalls and does a cursory check. "You're good to go, ma'am."

"Thank you." I smile at her because it's still in me to be polite. "I'll try not to take too long, but this dress is a little tricky."

She smiles back. "Trust me, I understand. Normally during my days I'm wearing pants and a button-down shirt. It was hard for me to get into this for tonight."

We share a laugh, understanding as only women can do before I quickly go inside.

As I'm doing my business, I hear her turning people away. Another thing I'll never get used to. No one is allowed to be in the bathroom when I am. When we're in public like this, I originally tried to hold it. In the beginning I held it until we got back to the castle, but now I understand that sometimes I need a moment from the public's eye. Surprisingly, it's not hard to get the dress off and back on. When I come out, she's waiting for me. She helps me wash my hands, and as I'm drying them off, I look at her. "Can you check to make sure I've got everything in its place."

"No problem. Turn around for me."

I do as asked. She gives me two thumbs up to let me know I've done well on my own. Hands washed, dried, and clothes in place, I tell her I'm ready to go back out.

She holds her finger up to advise me to hang on for a moment. When I nod that I understand, she goes out and presumably takes a look around. Seconds later, she's back inside, motioning for me to come on.

When we're back in the corridor, there are a few people milling around. I give them my most serene smile and nod. As we enter the ballroom, someone comes out at the same time, accidentally hitting me in the shoulder. My detail immediately stops them.

"I'm so sorry," the man says as he bows. "I wasn't watching where I was going."

"It's okay," I tell him. "No harm, no foul." But when he looks back up at me, his blue eyes are ice cold, and for once, I know exactly what the expression means about someone walking all over your grave. Our gazes hold as my detail turns me back toward my husband.

And as I sit down, I can feel his eyes on me, sending a shiver through my body.

Tristan looks over at me. "Are you cold?"

"No." I shake my head slightly. "Just a chill." But somehow this innocent meeting seems so much more than that.

CHAPTER 6
TRISTAN

We're trying to leave the ball, but there are cameras going off in every direction as we're making our way to our SUV. Holding Amelia close to me, I try to shield her from most of the flashes. Rain is coming down at a steady pace, and there are citizens lined up and down the streets.

"We should get to the SUV." Parker tries to direct us straight down the red carpet. "I don't like being out here in the open like this."

While I agree with him, there are thousands of people lined along the streets, and judging by how water-soaked they are, they've been there for a while. "We have to say hello to them," I argue with him. "It's what my mom would've wanted." And I know this more than anything else. My dad never wanted to stop and thank the community for their support. My mom was the soft to his hard, and she was always cognizant of the sacrifice the people of our country have made for us. Reaching out, I grab hold of Amelia's hand. "Do you want to go say something to them?"

Her eyes meet mine, and a small smile crosses her face. "Is that what you want to do? Is this how you want your monarchy to run? If it is, then I'm right there with you."

I'm unsure how to explain to her the type of leader I want to be, so

I say these words, "My mom would always make it a point to at least address the children. They've been waiting for who knows how long."

"Then that's what we'll do. I'm not afraid to get a little wet."

And neither am I.

Carefully we make our way across the street, an umbrella in my hand, shielding her as best I can. Parker is growling beside me, but I'm doing my best to ignore it. "You'll be fine," I say softly to him.

"Hopefully you will be too," he quips.

When we get to the other side of the street, there are loud claps and cheers. Ignoring the moisture on the ground, Amelia bends and smiles at a group of children. They hold out flowers to her, and she gratefully accepts them. "Thank you so much for waiting for me out here. I know it's cold and rainy."

The little girl grins at her. "It's going to snow soon. You look like a princess in your dress." She reaches out to finger the silky material.

Most people would probably shrink away, not wanting a child to touch such an expensive piece of clothing, but not Amelia. She leans into it.

"One day you'll have a dress like this. What's your name?"

"Chelsea. My mom says I have to learn not to drop food on my clothes first." She pouts. "I'm doing my best."

Amelia laughs before leaning in to give the little girl a hug. When she gets up, we make our way together down the line. I'm shaking hands, thanking everyone for being there, and Amelia has more flowers than she knows what to do with.

"We got married the same day you did," a couple says as they stand together, holding hands.

"Did you?" Lia smiles at them. "How exciting."

"It was great." He laughs. "There wasn't anyone on the streets, and we were able to walk into a pub and have a pint without waiting."

"We're happy we could help you with that," I say, reaching out to shake his hand. "What are your plans?"

They seem surprised that we're standing here talking to them, but this is an important piece of the way I want to rule my people. My mom was a queen of the people, and we lost that when we lost her. When I was younger, I didn't have an opportunity to be the type of person I know she wanted me to be because my dad was manipulative, and we had such a crappy relationship for the bigger part of my life.

"We're college students. We hope to finish our degrees and then buy a house and start a family."

That sounds like what I would be doing if I weren't the King of Haldonia. "It sounds like you have a good plan. If we can do anything to help, please let us know." I slip them a card with Parker's name on it. Hopefully, if we can be of help, they will reach out.

"Thank you, King Tristan."

Reaching over, I grab Amelia's hand in mine. The rain is coming down harder, and if we don't get out of it now, we might catch a cold, and neither of us wants that. "Are you ready?" I ask her.

She nods, pressing her lips into a smile. "You know I'll go anywhere with you."

Threading my fingers through her hair, I palm her nape and take the kiss I've wanted from her all night. It's right here in front of everyone, and I can't say that I even care.

Beside me, Parker is talking to someone through the microphone on his wrist. "You know that picture is going to be on the front page of every rag mag in the country, right?"

"I do."

And I can't help but be really excited about it.

"When are we leaving to go to the weekend house?" she asks as we scoot in.

"Hopefully tonight. There are a few things I need to do back at the castle, so I've asked them to take us there first. Then we can get my sports car to the weekend house if you'd like."

Her thigh is pressed tightly against mine, and she settles back into the leather seats of the SUV. "Before we got married, I'd read the articles about you and your sports cars. I'd see the pictures of you with them, and you'd look so hot. I've barely ridden with you anywhere other than on the back of your bike. I'm excited about this."

He seems amused. "I don't know that I understand, but if you're excited about it, then so am I. Parker, you're good with us going by the castle, right?"

"It's not my favorite thing, knowing that we'll be there almost completely alone, but if that's what you need to do, we will."

"What about Shannon?" Amelia asks. "Will she be riding back with us, too?"

Parker makes a noise in his throat. "Shannon will be riding with me as we follow the two of you in Tristan's car. I'll make sure she gets there safely."

Amelia and I share an amused smile. They think they're hiding everything from anyone who's watching, but they aren't. "You do what you have to do, Park. We'll be ready when you are."

He turns in the front passenger seat. "You act like you have a choice, Tristan. I have to follow you no matter where you go."

"But you act like I can't shake you, Park, and both of us know I've done it more than once."

He shakes his head, knowing I'm right and not to try me. Even though it's for the best, he's here to protect me. I do know how to take care of myself too.

"Are you two done playing whose ego is bigger?" Amelia asks, tucking her hand into the crook of my elbow.

"We're never done with that." I lean over and stamp a kiss against her forehead. "But we both know the winner is me."

She rolls her eyes, but she tilts her head so that it's resting on my shoulder. Here, in the back of this SUV, cocooned in the warm leather seats, I'm more content than I've ever been.

CHAPTER 7
AMELIA

I've never been in the castle with no one else really here before. It's kind of freaky how quiet it is, but at the same time, we're spending time alone and together. Tristan and I don't get enough of that as a pair of newlyweds.

Walking into his office, he has a seat behind his desk. It never fails to make my core clench as I look at him in that position of power. He's so hot sitting there, like he's able to command the country to do anything at the snap of his fingers.

"Why are you looking at me like that?" Tristan asks as he stares at me.

"I see you in different ways every single day. Sometimes you're my husband, other times you're my crush, my best friend, and then when you sit behind this desk? You're hotter than anyone else I've ever seen."

He grins. "What do you think when you see me back here?"

If only he knew, and do I really want to tell him? It gives him an advantage over me, one I'm unsure if I want to give him that power. "I see you as the strongest person I know. Most people would be scared to take over a country at your age. Even though you've been preparing for it your whole life, it's still overwhelming. How are you handling it?"

"No one has asked me that before." He scoots up closer to his desk and puts his hands on the polished wood. "Thank you for asking. I am overwhelmed. There are a lot of parts of the job I always assumed he wasn't very good at or that he didn't care about. Now I'm beginning to see there are a lot more issues at stake than him just wanting to make something happen. There are checks and balances in every part of our government. Even if I wanted to, I can't make the decisions I want to."

"How does that make you feel? It would make me frustrated."

"It does." He runs his fingers through his hair. "I had all these grand plans of the changes I was going to make. How I was going to come into office and within the first one hundred days I would let the people of Haldonia know they were cared for." He shrugs, grabbing a pen and clicking it off and on. "That's just not what's happened so far. I'm learning to temper expectations and take the small wins, ya know? It helps having you by my side."

"How's that?" I ask, laying my head down on the desk and gazing up at him. "I haven't done anything other than accept a bunch of invitations for us to appear in public. I feel as if I'm the one who's holding us back to make those changes."

"No." He shakes his head." I wish you'd known my mom. You remind me so much of her. She might have spent most of her life doing these same appearances you're talking about, but the people loved her. If there was anyone they wanted to see out in public, it was her. Anytime there was some sort of disaster, or a worry about the people of Haldonia, they would look to her, not my dad."

"And did she help them to feel better?"

His eyes get sad. "She helped me. I was never scared when she was around. If my mom was there, I knew there wasn't anything that would hurt me. I counted on her." He clears his throat. "And it killed me when she died. I wish she would have met you."

"I wish I would've met her too. Go ahead, and do what you need to. I'll be right here waiting for you. All I wanna do is watch you work."

He raises his eyebrows, but takes his jacket off, undoes the buttons on his shirt, and pushes them up past his elbows. My eyes watch him as he works, his brows furrowing as he reads a few pieces of paper and then scrawls his signature on them. I know what I do every day when I'm in my office, but I've always wondered what he does. It's not as if I think he's wasting his day doing nothing, but I have no idea what a king does in his office.

An hour later, he looks up to me. "Thanks for being patient. I'm ready to go if you are."

My stomach feels as if a bunch of small birds are flying around in it. "I can't wait to see your car, and I really can't wait to watch you driving it."

He reaches out to take my hand. "Let's go, Lia."

Little does he know I would follow him wherever he wants to go.

This is another thing I've never done. Been in the garage of the castle. I, of course, knew it was there, but I never had a reason to go there before, and I've never thought about going down there on my own.

"What all is in here?" I question as we ride the elevator down.

"Cars mostly, a couple of motorcycles, and a few vehicles that are special to the country. My mom's old car is down there. Sometimes I go sit in it. If I inhale deep enough, I can still smell her."

"Do you want to show me her car?"

There's a pride in his gaze I've never seen. "I'd love to show you her car."

When the elevator comes to a stop and we exit, he brings me over to a white Mercedes G-Wagon. "She was so regal in this thing." His voice is reverent. "I can still see her sitting tall in the seat. When she got this car, she was so excited to travel wherever she wanted to as long as security said it was okay."

It's been lovingly cared for, but I'm ready to see the car we'll be driving tonight. "Show me yours."

"Oh babe, I'll show you everything of mine."

The tone in his voice brings heat to my cheeks. "You know what I mean in this instance."

"I do, but let me introduce you to the baby I had before you." He struts over to the other side of the garage and hits a button. There, a sleek, black car that looks like the definition of sex sits before us. It's shiny. "This one is mine." He runs his hand across the hood, touching it like a lover. "Let's go, Lia. I wanna fly with you."

CHAPTER 8
TRISTAN

This is the first time in too long that I've had my car underneath me, going a hundred and fifty miles an hour. Beside me, Amelia has a huge smile spread across her face, and she's gripping the edge of her seat. When she squeals, I gun the engine again.

"You used to drive like this all the time?"

"All the time. I had a death wish. More than anything, I missed my mom, and I was sick of being without her. I didn't feel like my dad loved me, and I was struggling with it. The only thing I could think of was if I died like her, then he couldn't ignore me."

We're quiet as the road flies past us, when she speaks. "He was hurting just as much as you were, but you couldn't see it."

"No, I couldn't. Not back then, but now I do." Slowing down so that I'm no longer in the three-digit MPH, I feel comfortable enough to reach over and grab her thigh with my hand. Her dress is pulled up so that I can see the bare flesh. If Parker wasn't tailing us, I'd pull over to the side of the road and spend a few minutes showing my wife just how much I love and want her.

"You keep moving that hand of yours up, and I'm going to want you to do dirty things to me. Too bad we can't."

I make a noise deep in my throat as I think about what we could do together. "Who's to say we can't?"

"Tristan, it's dangerous."

"Lia, what have I just told you about myself? I love the thrill of the danger, and if I can have that with you, then I want it even more. So, if that's what you want too? Then sit back, spread your knees, and let me get you off."

She does as I've asked, and that part of my personality that still needs to be the bad boy? The rebel? In this moment I realize that with her, I'm able to be both.

AMELIA

The blunt tips of his fingers are teasing along the gusset of my panties. Frustrated and ready to feel his flesh against mine, I adjust so that he can rub at the edge of my pussy. Slowly he enters my folds, and I tilt my head back against the headrest.

With my eyes closed, I let the feeling wash over me.

"Lia, I'm ready for you to come for me. Right here against the leather of my seats. Every time I look over at that seat, I want to be able to think about this moment. Do you wanna come for me?"

I nod, pulling my bottom lip between my teeth. "Yes, I want to give both of us that memory."

He pulls his fingers from my core and puts them in his mouth, swirling his tongue around the digits. And then he puts them right back where they were. Spreading my knees as far as I can, I thrust toward him.

"Touch yourself, Lia. Make yourself feel good."

Since it's the dead of the night and I'm sure no one can see us, I reach up and grab my breasts, worrying the nipples behind the fabric of my dress. They're peaked and begging for his mouth. I wish I could pull the dress down and give him these parts of me, but it's too dangerous.

"We're about to hit the bridge to cross over to the island. It's up, and there are people standing outside, Lia. If you want to come, you have to do it now. I don't want anyone else to see what's mine."

My breath hitches as he twists his wrist and hits a spot inside my body I didn't know he could reach, and at that moment I fly apart.

CHAPTER 9
TRISTAN

Wrapping my arms around Amelia, I squeeze tightly. After the stress of the past few months, these are my favorite moments. When she and I can be together without the glare of everyone staring at us. Inside this house there's no one listening, and there aren't cameras or phones stretched toward us, hoping to catch some sort of secret.

Here, we can be ourselves.

It's the only place I've ever felt at home, and I'm lucky I get to be here with her. Kings Pass has my heart, and if I could, I would run Haldonia from here.

"Your feet are warm," she sighs as she cuddles deeper into my arms.

"Yours are cold, as always, but don't worry, I'll heat them up for you." I turn over, leaning in, and cuddling against her. It feels as if we haven't had many moments alone lately. The push and pull of being in charge of an entire country is even more than I thought it was. Not to mention she has her own responsibilities now. When we first met, she had a lot to learn with being my wife, but now that she wears the ring on her finger, it's increased tenfold.

"What's going on in that head of yours?" She runs her fingers down the side of my cheek. "I can hear you thinking over here."

I shake my head, giving her a small smile. "Just wondering if you'd like to take a ride with me today. It's been a while since we got on the back of my bike because it's been so cold."

"It has, and we both know there will probably be one more shot of winter before it's officially spring. In fact, I think I saw it might snow tomorrow when I was looking at the weather." She nibbles her bottom lip between her teeth.

"Then let's get out of here and do something fun today. Let's get out of this bed and breathe some fresh air." Until we started talking about coming up here, I didn't realize how badly I needed it. It isn't as if we don't come up here often. It's that I miss it so much.

If we were normal people without a monarchy counting on us, this is where we would stay all the time.

"Come on, Tris. Let's go. I'm dying to see you in that leather jacket and the helmet."

She sure does love the helmet. Reaching out, I grab her chin, yanking it down so that our eyes meet. "Lia, I have a feeling that if I wanted to fuck you wearing the helmet, you'd let me."

Her face heats, patches of pink appear on her cheeks. Those eyes of hers dilate, and she pokes her tongue out to lick her lips. "I would. We might be able to work that out if you'd like to."

Growling deep in the back of my throat, I tilt her chin down, taking her mouth with mine. It doesn't take much for us to lose ourselves in this kiss. Her mouth softens against mine as her arms wrap around my neck, thighs spread to make room for me between them. Smearing my nose down her neck, I take a nip at her collarbone before pulling back. "As much as I'd love to stay right here with you all day, I think we both decided we needed to get out and grab some fresh air."

She licks her lips, a smile spreading across her face. "Okay, but I'm asking for a rain check."

"You can bet your ass on that." I open my palm and slap it against the cloth-covered cheek of the ass I just talked about. "Let me go tell Parker what our plans are for the day, and then I'll get dressed."

"Looking forward to it."

"Are you sure this is a good idea?" Parker asks as I talk to him about what Amelia and I want to do for the day. "You know there's been some chatter on the official channels about an event."

"What event?"

No one ever wants to be honest with me. They want to dance around what the truth may be and expect me to make a decision on half-truths. Meanwhile I'm supposed to be protecting an entire country.

He raises his eyebrows and tilts his head toward me. "You know."

"Do I? You haven't told me what's being whispered behind my back. I've been waiting on it, Parker, but you're still beating around the bush." With my hands on my hips, I tilt my head back toward him. He's not the only one who can shame another person with a look. "If you really wanted me to know what's going on, you would've told me. Now I need you to tell me why Lia and I shouldn't take a day for ourselves."

He sighs. It's obvious in the way he doesn't meet my eyes that he doesn't want to tell me. "There have been a few issues."

I hate when he beats around the bush. "Why don't you tell me what those issues are, and then we can figure out how to deal with it."

"All right. Two weeks ago, the Haldonia security agency heard some chatter and intercepted a few messages that were of concern."

I don't like how this is sounding. Just like everyone else in our little country, I've lived through the attempted invasions. When I was a small child, there was an attempt to overthrow the government. Luckily for the last couple of decades, things have been quiet, but at the same time have we become complacent? "You need to tell me what this is about. I've mentioned to you I haven't felt comfortable. It's as if eyes are on me, which I know is stupid. All eyes are on me, regardless of if they're staring at me or not."

"You're right, and I should've been honest, but at the time, we weren't sure what was coming through."

Now this pisses me off. It's not often I get irritated with Parker. He's typically more honest with me than he probably should be, but my question is why this was kept from me. It's also time that we have a serious discussion about what I need to know at all times. "As your friend, I appreciate you not bothering me with what could be trivial. But as your king? This is a reprimand, Parker. To keep my country safe, to know what the proper protocols to follow are, and to answer any questions that anyone might have for me, I need to know what's going on. Even if you think it's not a credible threat, I need to know."

He looks as if he wants to argue but doesn't. "Yes, Your Majesty. Would you like a rundown of what we've discovered so far?"

"Do I need to worry?"

"Not right now. We don't believe it's to a point that you need to be concerned with yet. I'm just asking that you keep your eyes peeled. I'm not trying to keep you and the queen from doing anything. I simply want you to know that you should be more careful than normal."

I trust Parker with everything, from the moment he became the head of my security, and I'm not about to stop now. "Then we will, and if you feel as if you need to pull us, we'll go without argument. I do ask that you keep this from Lia until I get a briefing."

"Understood, sir."

I'm not the type of man who likes hiding things from his wife, but this is supposed to be a good weekend for us. It's supposed to be a weekend where we don't have to think about all the annoyances of daily life. "All right, the queen and I will be ready to go in the next thirty minutes. Expect me to ride the bike."

He nods. "Permission to be excused so that I can take care of securing the route."

"Please don't mention anything to Lia. I'll take care of what she needs to know after I've been debriefed."

"Yes, Your Majesty."

When Parker leaves, I glance out of the window, letting my gaze taken in the ocean below. It's tumultuous, as it normally is in the winter and spring. The waves are spinning together, making a run at the shoreline, before crashing into the rocks. The way it sloshes back and forth reminds me of my emotions. From happy to worried and then back again.

Never did I believe that becoming king would cause such a jumble of my emotions. I wasn't ready for it, and now I'm not sure if I ever will be.

CHAPTER 10
AMELIA

I love when Tristan and I take his bike down the coast. It's the one time where I don't feel as if we're on display. We both wear helmets, and while most everyone knows it's us, they don't take pictures and sell them to magazines or websites. We're allowed to be free and just who we are.

Grabbing my phone, I scroll so I can find what the weather is supposed to be today. It makes a big difference on what I'll be wearing. Sooner or later, I feel as if we'll move from these freezing temps to spring, but winter wants to hold on with its icy cold hands. When I see that it's cooler than I would like, I head over to my dresser and dig through it until I can find my favorite fleece-lined leggings.

"Is there anything I can do for you?"

I smile before turning around and facing Shannon. No matter how we started out together, she has morphed into the best personal assistant I could have ever asked for. Not to mention she's become a great friend. "Which pair of boots should I wear with my black fleece leggings?"

Her eyes brighten. The stylist in her misses those days where that's all she had to do, I'm sure. There's nothing she enjoys more than helping to dress me. "The moto ones that we bought a few months ago, when you explained to me how much you love riding the bike. Didn't you finally bring them up here a couple of weeks ago?"

"I did. They're in my closet."

Before I can make a move, Shannon is already heading to where I said they would be. I'm so used to being around her that I don't think anything about taking my pajama pants off and changing in front of her. Within a few minutes I have the leggings on, as well as a long sweater. She brings the boots over, along with a pair of thick socks.

"So, what are you and Tristan planning on doing today?" She makes the small talk, as I continue getting dressed.

"We're going up and down the coast, obviously. I'm hoping we can stop at the fish and chips place that I love and have a pint."

She laughs as she has a seat next to me. "If the country knew how normal the two of you are, they wouldn't believe it. It amazes me. Did I ever tell you I'd worked for another member of a monarchy before?"

"No, it's never come up, I don't guess." Now I'm interested as to why she didn't tell me. Shannon is not the kind of person to keep secrets, so there must be a reason.

She nods, rolling her lips together. A sigh works its way out of her chest, and she turns to face the window. It looks out over the same ocean that can be seen from most of the house. Although the rolling waves are in chaos, they calm down whoever is looking out at them. It's one of the things I love most about this house, well other than the fact not everyone can get here. "I worked for the Calder family."

I shiver when she mentions that name. The Calders of Crona are the mortal enemies of Haldonia. Over the last century they have tried to invade no less than five times. "You worked for them?" I'm shocked. This isn't something we've ever discussed.

"It's where I was born and raised, but when it came to staying there indefinitely, I couldn't do it."

"How long did you work for them?" I take a seat on the bed and put the boots on.

"Four months. That was as long as I could handle it. There were so many things I saw that I know I would never see here, in Haldonia."

I've always been curious as to what happens in the country to our east, but I've never been able to ask. It's been forbidden. "Like what? How bad are they, really?"

She swallows, her throat moving up and down with the force of it. The normally bright eyes are shadowed and dull. This isn't who I'm used to seeing, and it worries the hell out of me. "They're some of the worst I've ever seen. I've lived my life in fear that they'll interrupt the peaceful existence I've managed to build."

I'm quiet as I watch, waiting for her to confide in me. We've grown close since she became my stylist and then my personal assistant. There's nothing she hasn't seen in the last few months when it comes to us. Maybe I shouldn't have been so open, but I needed at least one person I could trust unconditionally besides my husband. My heart pounds against my chest as I wait for her to speak. I've never been this nervous before, not even when I first met Tristan.

What if she's about to confide that she's screwed me over? It takes everything I have not to speak before she does, but I wait it out.

"For a while it seemed as if they were nice. Not like the two of you, but slightly comparable. It wasn't until I had been there for a few weeks, before I started to notice things seemed off."

She looks as if she needs a little prompting, so I give her a little. "Like what?"

"When I first started, they introduced me to their daughter. She was four and the cutest little girl I'd seen. There was nothing that didn't put a smile on her face. Happiness was contagious when she was around. One day, she stopped smiling, her eyes were dark, and she withdrew into herself. Sometimes I saw bruises, and I asked her about it. She refused to speak about it, but I kept on."

I reach out, grabbing her hand with mine. "Of course you did. You're a great person, and you were obviously worried about her. Did she ever confide in you?"

Shannon nods, tears pooling in her eyes. "Five days before I left, she came running to my bedroom, quietly knocking on the door. At first, I wasn't sure I'd actually heard the sound or not. Then I heard it again. So, I went investigating."

I'm terrified of what she's going to tell me. "This is going to break my heart, isn't it?"

She nods, her nose and eyes red as she tries to fight back her emotions. "I pulled her into my room and drug her over to the bed. When I sat her down, there was blood on her hands and arms. I kept looking for where it was coming from, and when I couldn't find it, I asked her."

"Please tell me she wasn't sexually assaulted."

"She wasn't, but she took my hand and lead me down the hallway to her mom's room. Her mom and dad didn't share, which I always thought was odd, especially since I've seen how close you and Tristan are. We went to the bathroom, and that's where she was. She'd been beaten." Shannon wipes under her eyes. "Badly."

"Oh, I hate this for you and her. How do you trust someone after they've done this to you?"

"You don't," Shannon cries. "Or you don't, if you're allowed to. I kneeled down and asked if I could help her. She shook her head, holding her lips so firm, her chin so strong. I told her a few times that it was okay, she could break down if she needed to, no one would think bad of her. Not me, not her daughter, but she refused."

It hits me hard that she was used to this. "Because it's normal for her, and she knew she'd have to be standing next to her husband at whatever event they had after this." I'm broken up about this too, because I'd been so worried about who Tristan would be. The type of man he was, and how he would treat me. I was prepared for whatever would come my way, but there was a part of me that knew I wouldn't be able to take someone controlling me lying down.

"Exactly. It happened again twice in the next week, and then I saw a woman I'd never seen running from her husband's room with tears streaming down her face. I tried to stop her, but she wasn't ready for it. That's when I started paying attention to everything that was happening around them." Her shaking fingers run through her hair. "Most everyone who was around them? It was as if they were walking around in some sort of stupor, as if they weren't aware of what was going on in their lives."

"Like they were drugged?" This is sounding worse and worse.

"I wasn't sure. Still not, really." She sighs, blowing out a breath. "All I knew was I had to tell someone, and I did."

Now I'm invested in this. "What did they do? Who did you tell?"

"I told the head of security, because I was worried something was happening to the royal family, not within it, necessarily. After I told them, I approached it as an outsider, of course, because that's who I was. I watched and waited, sure that there would be changes within the organization, but there wasn't." She rolls her lips together before pulling the bottom one between her teeth.

"As if they knew what was going on and that there was no reason to be concerned?" I supply for her, thinking about why that would be.

"Exactly. When I realized they weren't going to do anything, and I'd potentially put myself in danger by basically blowing my own cover, I left. For a while I drifted, and then my boss came to me and asked if I'd be willing to help you. I wasn't sure at first."

Can't blame her for that. "I'm glad you took a chance, Shannon, but I need you to be completely honest with me. Why did you mention this?"

She leans in, dropping her voice an octave. "Because I feel like I'm being watched. At first it didn't seem weird, because the entire world's eyes are on you. But..." Her eyes dart back and forth in the room. "It seems stronger lately."

This is where I should tell her the same. "I know what you mean, but I haven't wanted to bring attention to it."

"So it's not just me?"

I shake my head. "I've felt it too. Promise me if you see something, you'll say something."

She reaches out, hugging me tightly. "I will if you promise, too."

"All right." I sigh, wiping at the surprising tears under my eyes. "I need to get dressed and go meet Tristan. He's going to wonder where I've been."

We share shaky smiles, and I tell myself that I'm going to have fun today. Not worry about what tomorrow might bring.

CHAPTER 11
TRISTAN

At the back of my mind, I'm worried. It's a nagging at the skin on my neck. As if it's like an itch I just can't reach. Not because of everything Parker confided in me, but because Amelia was late coming down from our room. When I saw her, she wasn't smiling like she normally is, and there's a worry shining brightly deep in them. The fact she didn't immediately tell me what's bothering her makes me worry more. Taking a deep breath and letting it out, I try to relax.

We're still learning about one another, and perhaps this is something she can't tell me yet.

"Are you ready?" I ask her, motioning out to the bike. I'm anxious to get going. The longer we're in here, the more we're running out of time to spend together.

"Yup, just let me grab my jacket."

My eyes track as she takes long strides toward the closet we keep them in. Her legs are impossibly long, although she's on the shorter side. Closing my eyes, I can imagine them wrapped around me and the serene smile on her face.

"Tristan? What are you thinking about?"

Smirking over at her, I answer, "Wouldn't you like to know?"

Her eyes flitter down below my waist, catching what I know is a slightly hard cock. It's no surprise. It always is around her. "I think I already do." She reaches out, grabbing the waistband of my pants. "Let's go, Tris. Otherwise we're not going to leave."

She's damn right about that. Cupping my palm around the curve of her ass, I slap it, causing her to jump and a cute little surprised gasp to escape her lips. Digging my fingers through her hair, I wrap it around my fist and yank back. It exposes her neck to my lips, and I take advantage, smearing my kiss up to her jawline. "I love you, Lia. Don't ever forget that."

"I won't." With a turn on her heel, she's out the door, and I'm following her like a lost puppy.

Typically, getting on my bike and this drive are the best things to settle my nerves, but today the silence in my ears because of the helmet is disconcerting. When I see a turnoff up ahead, I make a hasty decision and pull onto the gravel. It's an outlook we've never been to before, and if I can, I'll use it as an excuse to get her to talk to me.

When I come to a stop, I steady the bike so she can get off.

We glance out at the steady waves on this side of the island, and I look over at her. "Why were you so quiet when you came downstairs? There was a troubled look on your face, and I'm just wondering what happened. I know I didn't ask you then, but I didn't want to start our ride off on a bad note."

She sighs heavily, raising her shoulders in question. "I was talking to Shannon, and a few things that we were discussing struck me as odd and worrisome, if I'm being completely honest."

Her tongue comes out to lick her lips. Then there's a tell, she pulls her hair back into a ponytail, holding it with her hand. She only does this when she's nervous. It's a way to keep her hands busy and her eyes away from anything that will allow me to tell what she's really thinking. "What are you worried about?"

"Did you know Shannon used to work for the Calders?"

This isn't news to me, but I play it off. "I didn't, but I'm sure that she was checked out before she was allowed around us. Parker always makes sure we're safe."

"Yeah."

But there's still some wariness in her.

I wrap my arms around her neck and pull her in close before dropping a kiss on her forehead. "You're not worried? Not about Crona?"

She wraps those arms around my waist and snuggles in close.

I try not to let her know that I am. My advisers have also been talking about Crona, and the fact that she's mentioning it worries me a lot. "What did she tell you about it?"

"She ended up leaving because she didn't trust them. She's never discussed it before. Not that I don't trust her, because I do. I trust her with everything. But it just struck me as odd that we've never discussed it. What else do I not know about her?"

My wife looks up at me, as if she wants me to tell her, but I let her keep talking. She's the smartest person I know when she's talking things out on her own. But there are secrets I have.

"I feel as if that's my responsibility as her queen—to know about her life and to question the things she did before. When I heard her say that, I did a double take."

I would've too, and now that stress I was hoping to get rid of is back with a vengeance. To loosen myself up, I move my neck back and forth, listening as it cracks and sighing with relief.

At that moment, her eyes turn to me, accusatory. "You knew, didn't you? I can't explain it, but my intuition says you knew."

Honesty goes a long way, and I know that about marriage, so I'm going to give her a little so that she'll trust me when it's imperative. "I knew about it. I know about everything."

"Why didn't you tell me, Tristan?" The tone of her voice is disappointed, and I hate to know I'm the person that caused it to be there.

"Because it didn't really have anything to do with you. At the end of the day, it's my decision, with Parker's approval, who works with you. You get to choose. I give you the people to choose from." This doesn't make me feel good, to be manipulative, but there's so much I have to keep secret from everyone. She needs to know how much I care for her. "I'm not going to give you someone who's going to harm you. I hope you know that. I love you. If you got hurt, I would never forgive myself."

There's a moment of silence between us that could turn awkward, but it doesn't. Instead, she inhales deeply and holds my hands with hers. I wait for her to speak and give her my full attention.

"I appreciate you taking care of me. No one else has ever done that. Not like you." With her hand, she releases mine and then runs her palm down my cheek and neck. I lean into it as she begins talking again. "I just felt blindsided."

There's a part of me that doesn't want to broach this subject, but I know I must. She needs to understand her place in the grand scheme of things. "You are my wife, and I respect you. I will respect you every step of the way. I hope you understand that. At the same time, there are going to be things I have to keep from you because I am the King of Haldonia. And there are going to be things that I have to take to my grave, Amelia—things I can't tell you about."

She tilts her head to the side, nodding. With the way she's chewing on her lip, she wants to say something. Somehow, she keeps it in while I continue.

"Not that I don't want to, but it's important. There are issues and threats to this country. I have to keep up on that. I have to keep you safe, the country safe, myself safe. If I'm out here blabbing everything I hear, that's not going to happen. I hope you understand."

She smiles softly. "I do. I do, and I know all of this. Sometimes I just have to remind myself our marriage isn't exactly normal."

"I'm sorry. I know how you feel. There were times when I was a teenager when I had to hold secrets from my best friends. It hurt, especially when I could protect them. This"—I gesture between the two of us—"doesn't make me feel any better. Can we please have a good afternoon together?"

There's a part of me that wants to tell her what I know. There's another part of me that wants to keep her in the dark, but I know after this discussion she's not going to go for it.

"We can."

I tilt her chin down with my thumb and forefinger. "Enjoy this day,

Lia. It might be one of the last ones we have for a while. Interpret that however you wish."

Her eyes pool with tears and realization spreads across her face. I've told her, without telling her. "Let's go." She reaches her hand out to mine. "We're going to have a great day."

"That we are."

She giggles as I chase her along the beach. On this side of the island, it's not covered in rocks. There's flat sand, and although it's cold, we're having a great time. Her dark hair whipping around her body teases me as I chase behind her. Once I catch up to her, I hook my arms around her waist and take her down, my body covering hers. The smile that's been spread across her face is wiped away, replaced with a seriousness that causes my chest to tighten. "You're beautiful."

"You're trying to flatter me," she whispers. "So that you can get my clothes off."

She knows me better than anyone else. When we were approached about our arranged marriage, this was the part I was worried about. Would we know each other? Really know one another? The way couples who have been together for years do? Just because we were introduced not long before our marriage, I still wanted us to be like my parents.

Turns out, we have been, and I love it.

"I don't think I have to flatter you to get your clothes off, Lia."

Licking her lips, she flutters her eyes down. "You're right, you don't. It would take a lot less for me to take my clothes off for you, although maybe not here."

I'm pulled back to the present. She makes me forget everything. Where we are, who can see, and that I'm the king of a fucking country and should conduct myself as such.

CHAPTER 12
AMELIA

Cooking breakfast is one of the things we love the most when we come to our weekend house. It allows us to be ourselves without knowing others are watching, and I find that Tristan is much more playful.

He'll put a dollop of whipped cream on my nose and lick it off, or he'll come strolling into the dining room stripping his clothes off and flashing his abs to my hungry eyes. No matter how often I see him, I want to see more.

I think back to the first time we were here and the pancakes we made. It's one of the reasons we're making pancakes right now. He's stirring them as if his life is depending on it. Glancing over Tristan's shoulder, I remark, "That's really thick. You should probably thin it out a little bit."

He turns his head over his shoulder, giving me a wink. "That's what she said."

I throw my head back, laughing. "If only the people of this country knew how dirty your mind was and how well you can take a joke."

"Take a joke? I can fucking land one too." He slaps his hand down on the counter. "I wish I could be this way with everybody." He shakes his head thoughtfully. "But so many don't want this side of me. The few times I've tried, all I've heard is I'm the king, and I should take things seriously. So I've been trying to keep this piece of my personality to myself."

I hate that for him. He's one of the funniest people I know. It's one of the ways he keeps the stress at bay, and I've never known him to do it at inappropriate times, but I guess he's been called out for it. If I would give him anything, it would be the freedom to be exactly who he is.

Wrapping my arms around his waist, I dig my forehead into his back. "This is my favorite part of you. The one who doesn't take himself too seriously, and definitely the one who shows me who he is outside of his office."

He makes a noise deep in his throat before he hooks his arm around, pulling me to the front of his body. When we're facing one another, he drops his forehead down to mine. "I love to show you who I am every time and anytime we're out of anywhere, so if you ever need me to remind you, please let me know."

I lift on my toes and press our lips together. The kiss quickly gets out of hand, and I'm reminded that we only have a little time here— not much at all, really.

"Tris," I whisper, "do we really want the breakfast?"

He growls. "I'm good with saying fuck it if you are."

"Let's do it."

I squeal as he lifts me up and throws me over his shoulder in a fireman's carry. The fact that he's strong enough to do this is really a turn on. He makes sure to turn off the stove and then carries me up the stairs.

When we get to the bedroom, he drops me on the bed, his eyes fierce and seductive. They rake over my body, causing my nipples to tighten and my pussy to clench. I spread my thighs to give him room to work. Before I know it, my clothes and his are off. His naked body moves against mine. His muscles rub my softer skin, causing goose bumps to appear.

"Tris, that feels good," I moan as his lips move from my chin, down to my throat, and suck at my flesh.

"Damn right it does," he groans as he pulls away.

His cock on my thigh leaves behind a trail of liquid, and it excites me knowing that I affect him this way. Every time we're together like this, I'm amazed. I never imagined someone would want me like this man. Hooking my foot around his calf, I use it for leverage to turn him over onto his back.

"What are you doing?" he asks, his voice deep and full of desire.

God, this is the way I love him, so crazy for me, he can't hold back. "You know I love to ride."

A sexy smirk spreads across his face, before tilting the side of his mouth up. "That I do, but typically it's a motorcycle, and not my dick."

I throw my head back, laughing at him. "Hold on, Your Majesty. I'm gonna take care of you."

He dips his head into his chest. "You know me, I'll do whatever my wife tells me."

Reaching behind me, I grab hold of his cock at the base and hold it steady while I sink down. The feel of his body filling mine is enough to give me even more goose bumps. Reaching forward, I grab hold of the headboard, using it to help me move up and down on top of him. He thrusts up into me as I drop down onto him.

His hands come up to my breasts, cupping them in his palms. My nipples peak against the skin, running straight through my body, down to my core. Rocking back and forth on my knees, I shake slightly as he hits the spot that makes me come apart.

"Tristan, I love when you do that."

He groans. "I know you do." With a grunt, he holds my hips down to his, and with the strongest stomach muscles I've ever seen, he flips me over so that he's on top.

"Tris, shit..."

He pulls out, flipping me over onto my stomach. "Hands back on that headboard, Lia. You're gonna need to hang on tight."

I sigh, dropping my head as he thrusts in and then pulls out. His hands are rough on my hips, pulling me back and forth against him.

"Your pussy is gripping me so tight, Lia. Don't stop, and I won't."

"Please don't," I beg. One of his hands drops to the front of my body, his finger strumming my clit as he fucks me hard. This is what I love about how he takes me. He's not scared to make me break apart.

He buries his head in my back as he plays my body like a violin.

Opening my mouth, I scream as he takes me over the peak and explodes inside me.

Together we ride out the orgasm, our sweaty bodies sliding together. In this moment, I know I'll never be closer to Tristan than I am right now.

CHAPTER 13
TRISTAN

It's Monday, and I'm back in the office after our long weekend away. I wish that Amelia and I could spend unlimited time at the weekend house. To us, it's home. It's where we're happy, where we don't have the responsibilities of this country weighing down on us. But unfortunately, this is what I'm supposed to do. It's what I signed up for and what I was born into.

Today there's a weird kind of heaviness around the office and hallway leading to it. It's unusual because as an office, we're typically closer than this. We would normally be asking one another how the long weekend went. Instead, it's tense. There aren't any jokes, no smiles and laughs. If someone were to ask me what's different about this Monday compared to the others, I can't put my finger on it.

Turning around, I gaze out over the kingdom. What is everyone else doing today? What are their pressing issues? I wish I knew why it's at the forefront of my mind today. Again, it's another thing I can't quite put my finger on.

There's a knock at the door. The only one who knocks like this is Parker. "Come on in."

When he crosses the threshold from the hallway into the office, his mouth is set in a firm line.

Immediately, my stomach drops, because he isn't one to sugarcoat anything. But the way his jaw is set is scaring me.

"I don't have great news," he begins, rubbing his palms together.

I've been waiting on this, debating what he's going to say after what he let slip this weekend. None of this feels good. It's like we're on the edge of a great cliff, and it's only going to take a little push for us to fall.

"Okay, okay," I sigh, ready to hear what he has to say. Delaying it isn't going to make it much easier. "What is it? We need to know. So just lay it out for me. No matter how bad it is, or if you think it isn't a credible threat. Now's the time to work on a plan."

He opens his mouth to speak, and that's when the ground beneath us is rocked. I'm shocked. We're not on a fault line, and there's no volcano around. Absolutely no reason for the ground to be shaking like this, or the building we're in to be swaying back and forth. We've never had an earthquake in Haldonia before, so I'm confused about what's happening right now.

When my brain comes back online, I can smell acrid smoke, hear screams that are reverberating off the sides of the rooms, and what sounds like an audible gasp from the kingdom.

"What the fuck happened?" I yell, but my ears are ringing. Parker's laying over in the corner, blood pouring from a wound on his head, and the only thing I can think about is getting to Amelia. She's down the hallway in her office.

What in the world just fucking happened?

Scrambling over debris, I pick my way through the rubble, checking on Parker first. "Parker, are you okay? Wake up for me, man." I slap his face. With the first one, his eyes snap open.

"What happened?"

"That's what I'm asking myself, but I have to get to Amelia. She was down the hallway whenever this happened. What is it?"

He stays low but raises his head. "It's a bomb, Tristan."

A bomb? Someone bombed Haldonia. "What the fuck are you talking about?"

"The information I had to give you was about this. We'd gotten intel that Crona was going to try and invade Haldonia. I'd gotten it right before I came into your office." He coughs, the office seeming to fill up with more smoke than before.

These motherfuckers have decided to threaten my country? I still haven't laid eyes on my wife, and if there's a hair hurt on her head, I will end them. Before I can do anything, though, we have to get out of this office and into the basement of the castle. Because I know protocol, I look at Parker. "You're not getting me out of here before we get Lia. You can fucking forget it."

"King, you know who my vow is to. You're aware of my job, I know you are."

But he's torn. It's right there in the gleam of his eyes. He wants to go check on her, and we're both aware that isn't the way things are supposed to go down. "And I'm telling you, as your king, to go check on my fucking wife."

"I hear you, but only if you promise to listen to me. If you ignore one of my orders, you're done."

At this point I'll agree to anything he tells me I have to. "Let's go."

"Stay behind me."

I'd prefer to be in front of him, since he's still bleeding from the head, but since that's not an option here, I do as he asks. We stay low, and he pulls a gun from his coat that I didn't even know he carried. There's probably a bunch of things he has on him that I have no idea about. Stupidly, I never thought about it. My safety and security have always been a little of an afterthought to me. Now? It's at the forefront of my mind.

He doesn't say anything, instead he uses hand signals. I know what they look like, because I've been taught them once or twice, plus they're pretty self-explanatory. The closer we get to Lia's office, the more my heart is pounding. Sweat pours down my back and off my face, and my hands are shaking as I touch his suit jacket to make sure I don't lose him in the melee of what's going down. People are running this way and that, some of them have improvised masks, holding them over their faces. None of them are Lia though.

Parker comes to a stop and orders me to do the same behind him. He reaches out to touch the doorknob. I don't know if he's testing to see if it's hot or loose, but apparently he gets what he's looking for.

Turning the knob, he places his gun in front of him. When he's swept the entrance, he says back to me. "Clear. Come on."

When we get inside, that's where I see Amelia. She's curled up in a ball against the wall and shaking like a leaf. But my girl? She's holding a letter opener up like she's willing to fight the entire army to save herself.

Crawling over the carpet, I get to her and take her in my arms. "I'm here. We're together, and you're fine."

She breathes a sigh of relief, wrapping her arms around my neck. "Never let go, Tristan. Never let go."

CHAPTER 14
AMELIA

If someone were to ask me what I thought my life would be like married to Tristan, everything before five minutes ago would be the answer. My hope was that we'd live a great life, one full of love, happiness, and contentment. We were well on our way to that, and I believed, perhaps foolishly, that our love was destined to be grand and fairytale-esque.

Now? The floor beneath me has literally been shaken, and with it, my belief in everything. In the snap of a finger or the blink of an eye, life has changed. I never fully believed that was possible when others said it, but today, I've realized exactly what it means.

I'm holding on tightly to Tristan's hand. He's my anchor in the middle of this storm. My voice breaks as I ask, "What are we going to do?"

He reaches out, grabbing my chin with his fingers, and yanks it down so that our eyes meet. His voice is firm and leaves no room for argument. "We're going to survive. Whatever Parker tells us to do, we're going to follow him. He's going to get us out of this and make sure we're safe."

Swallowing roughly, I nod. My heart is pounding against my chest, my hands are shaking. I entwine my fingers with his, using that strength to turn to Parker and speak as clearly to him as I can. "Okay, Parker, tell us what to do."

He glances around the room, seeming to take in who all he has here and what he's working with. There's not much, but I'm willing to fight for my life as hard as I'm going to fight for Tristan.

His eyes stop on Shannon, and I watch as they have a conversation without words. Although he reaches forward, he doesn't actually touch her. I can't imagine being the two of them, not able to spend a few moments together in the middle of all of this destruction. He firms himself up and turns to us. "You all listen to me and listen now. I don't know what's down that hallway. There's no way to know what we're facing. Reinforcements have been called, but I can't be sure when they will get here. My main concern is making sure we get to the basement."

"Where the bunker is?" Tristan squeezes my fingers, giving me hope that we're going to get there safely.

"Exactly. The other members of Parliament should've proceeded in that direction, and once we've got everyone safe, we'll be able to discuss our next steps. There is a plan in place for a situation like this. We're going to follow protocol, and you're all going to get there with no problem."

He seems to speak his wishes into existence.

The tension in the room is thick. All of us know we're facing the unknown.

There's no way to know what's waiting on us outside this door. Absolutely no way of knowing if they've not only just bombed us but also infiltrated the castle. It's like we're in the scariest of haunted houses, and we're all waiting on a jump scare.

My heart breaks for Tristan and me. After starting our marriage with what appeared to be a fairytale, this has thrown a wrench in it all. Regardless of what I'd assumed and the history that encompasses this position, I'd been lured into a sense of false security. It had felt like no one would touch us, and we'd live a charmed life.

Now I can see how wrong that was. How naïve I was to think nothing could touch us. Just because we were the heads of a country didn't mean that we were untouchable. In actuality, it meant that we were a target, and I never even realized it. Parker is speaking again, and I force myself to listen intently, not wanting to be the person who fucks this up.

His voice is firm and doesn't have any room for anyone to question his words. "We're staying together, keeping low, and you're going to follow me as we travel through this hall. Tristan, I want your hand on my shoulder at all times. Shannon…" His eyes float over to hers, and the fear in them is palpable. "I need you to bring up the rear."

Her throat moves up and down as she swallows. "The priority is the monarchy. They'll be safe with me." She pulls a gun from a waistband that I've never seen before and pulls the slide back. "I got one in the chamber, and knowing how to shoot was in the job description. They're not getting past me, Park."

What in the fuck is happening here? How did I never know that my assistant was strapped and knew how to do some of the things that Parker does?

She motions with the gun. "Your hand on Tristan's shoulder the entire time. Tristan, her hand comes off, you yell."

I turn to her, the fear in my voice as I speak. "What about you? If your hand comes off my shoulder?" She's become my best friend. I don't want to think about what will happen to me if she's not here any longer. I want someone to reassure me we won't leave her behind.

Her eyes meet mine. They're shining brightly with unshed tears, but her tone and face are strong, and they say do not question what she's saying. "Then you go, and you don't look back. Listen to me. You don't worry about what happens to me. The priority is you and Tristan. I knew that when I signed on to do this job, Amelia. You're my friend, and I'll protect you to the very end."

I hate this. Shannon has been my friend, and she just referred to me as hers. We've laughed and cried. She's heard my secrets, and I've listened to hers. This isn't supposed to be happening, and I want to shout at God. Question why we're having to deal with this now. We've never hurt anyone, that I'm aware of.

On the verge of a breakdown, tears pool in my eyes, and I have to firm up my lips to keep them from falling. Now isn't the time to have emotions. It will only slow us down. Reaching out, I grasp her fingers in mine and squeeze, hoping that the small gesture conveys my fear, support, and thankfulness. She's putting her life on the line and doesn't seem to be thinking twice about it.

"Okay, everyone. Let's head out," Parker says. "I'll be using hand gestures. If you don't know what they are, use your context clues. I hate to be an asshole, but we don't have time. There's no way we can stop and answer questions. The priority is getting to the bunker and making sure everyone is safe."

My heart pounds as he opens the door, and we ease out. We no longer have the coverage of the room we're in. Out in the open, anyone can do anything, and that's got me terrified. We might as well have a target on our backs, but then again, we already do.

I've never been so tense or scared in my life. My shoulders shake as I stay hunched over between them. What's going to happen if I move the wrong way and we get caught? If us getting hurt is my fault, I don't know if I'll ever be able to forgive myself. In all the time I was coached to be the wife of a king, this was never talked about, and I'm wholly unprepared for all of this.

All I want to do is close my eyes and transport to the basement, to the safety I know is awaiting us. I don't want to have this uncertainty gnawing at my gut. This fear making my hands shake and legs feel as if they don't want to move me down the hallway. It takes a monumental effort for me to advance.

"C'mon, Amelia, you can do this," I whisper to myself. I've never been so terrified in my life

"You can," Shannon says softly. "I'm behind you, and I will make sure we get you to that basement, Amelia. Let's go. Close your eyes if you have to. I'll direct you. I'm not going to let anything happen to you. Besides Parker, you're the best friend I've ever had."

I give in to her advice, closing my eyes and trusting that the three people around me will get me to where I need to go. In the darkness, Tristan's hand finds mine again, and he squeezes, giving me the strength I can't seem to muster for myself.

It feels like an entire day as we slowly make our way down the hallway. When we come to a stop, I open my eyes. Parker looks back to us. "We have to cross the corridor. I'll be covering you all. Shannon is going to go first."

My heart is in my throat as I watch her scramble across the wide-open space. Once she gets to the other side, I feel as if I can breathe again.

"Okay, you two go together." Parker pushes us, not giving us time to second-guess what we're doing.

Dipping my head, I pray to God we're going to make it through this. For the first time in my life, I'm not sure we will.

CHAPTER 15
TRISTAN

When we get to the basement of the castle, I can finally take a deep breath and partially relax. Here, I feel safe. Can't say it's as if nothing can touch me here, but underground and with the stone walls around us, I'm able to get my mind right and try to form a plan for what's going to get us out of this mess.

There's a seat at the head of a long conference table. It's mine, and I'm expected to take it. But first, I have to make sure Amelia is okay. I hold up a hand, gesturing for them to give me a minute.

My eyes meet Amelia's from across the room, and I head over to her, holding my arms out. She collapses into them, holding on to me tightly. "I love you," I whisper. "We're going to figure this out."

"I love you too." She runs her fingers through my hair.

Pressing our foreheads together, I inhale her scent and allow it to calm me down. "Wait for me."

"Always."

This is the first time I've sat in front of the members of my cabinet like this. We haven't had a chance to get together and speak about situations at length. It's what I would have chosen to do if given the option. Instead, we don't have an option, and we've been forced to answer. Walking to the front of the table, I bend down, pressing my hands against the polished surface. I take a moment to look every member in the eye and give them a firm nod. When I speak, I make sure my voice doesn't shake. "As you all know, we were attacked a few minutes ago. We're still gathering information, and I will address the nation as soon as possible. Is everyone safe down here? Have any of you been injured?"

There are murmurs that go up along the room. Everyone seems to be checking in with each other.

When I'm satisfied that everyone around us is okay, I continue. "We won't sit back and not answer this. We may be a small nation, but we are strong. I plan to fight right alongside our forces." Raised voices go up around us. "If I'm going to ask the people of this country to fight for our future, then I'm going to do it as well. I'll be meeting with General Robinson after I leave here. By the end of the night, I will address Haldonia. But first, we need to take a vote. Are we all in agreement that Haldonia will answer this declaration of war, in kind?"

The vote goes through, and it's verified we'll answer the declaration of war. When we finish with the vote, I meet with some advisers as I craft what I'm about to say to the people of Haldonia. Over in the corner, Amelia and Shannon are standing there, trying to stay out of the way, but paying attention to what's happening.

When I can finally get away for a few moments, I walk over to my wife and take her in my arms. "I'm sorry I've had to leave you."

"It's okay." She leans her head against my chest. "You're about to tell me you're going to go, aren't you?"

"I am. This is my country, my duty, and I'm not going to sit by and let Crona fuck us over. We did absolutely nothing to them. This was an act of war. There's no other way to define it. They want our natural resources, and I'm not giving them up."

She hooks her arms around my waist. "I don't want you to, but I do want you to be careful. They'll come gunning for you because you're the king. I'm worried they won't be able to keep you safe."

I'm worried about that too, but I can't say it to Amelia. If I do, she'll worry, and it's important she stays strong for both of us. I'll need her strength to draw on once I'm in the field. "I'll have the best security out there. The entire army will be behind me, Lia."

"I know. Just promise me."

Dropping a kiss to her forehead, I whisper. "I promise."

My hands are shaking, and my palms are sweaty as I sit at the end of the table, waiting to speak to the people of Haldonia. I've never had such an important address to make. Waiting for them to tell me that I'm live on the air is like waiting for another bomb to drop. There's a loud ticking in my ears, and I'm afraid I'm going to pass out. Just as I'm about to ask them how much longer I need to wait, Shannon is motioning for me to go. I clear my throat and look dead ahead at the camera.

"People of Haldonia, I'm coming to you from a safe and undisclosed location. I'm here to assure you that we will answer Crona in kind. War has been declared, and we will be fighting it with the best forces in this part of the world. They will not defeat us. It will take sacrifice for all of us, including my family. Many of you will be saying goodbye to members of your family as they go to fight this battle."

My gaze moves to where Amelia is standing over to the side, regal as the queen she is. I'm fighting not just for this country, but for her and our future. She offers me a small smile.

"We will count on those of you who stay on the home front for support and encouragement. It will be a focal point of our campaign. Our first and foremost objective will be securing safety for our country. Once we close our border, allied forces will answer the attack that was perpetrated on Haldonia. We request your support and prayers as we protect this country."

There are so many emotions flowing through my body as I try to keep my voice steady. I manage to hold it together until Shannon motions that the broadcast is done. Once I know it's over, I turn away from everyone and let some of those emotions go.

"Tristan, you did amazing. I'll be here," Amelia says, grabbing my hands in hers. "Whenever you can come back to me, I'll be here."

"I love you, Lia. I'm not sure when I'll be able to contact you, but

I'll make sure that you know I'm okay. Hopefully, there will be times when I can get away and visit."

"Be safe." She wraps her arms around me, hugging tightly.

"Come with me." I grab her arm and pull her with me, along a corridor. I send a glance over at Parker, letting him know that I don't want to be bothered. I take her into the room and slam the door before flipping the lock.

This is the last time I'm going to be with her in the foreseeable future, and I'm about to take it.

CHAPTER 16
AMELIA

I've never seen this room before, didn't even know it was here. When he pulls me in behind him, I wrap my arms around his waist and hold on tight, burying my mouth in his neck. Inhaling deeply, I commit this scent to memory. Something I can hang on to in the dark nights when I'm missing him. "Tris, I'm terrified you're not going to come back to me," I cry.

"Hey, I'm going to come back to you. There's nothing that will be able to stop me."

A bullet will. A gun, or someone who wants to have the reputation of saying they got rid of the King of Haldonia. But I don't say any of this, not out loud, because I don't want to put that out into the world. "I know. Can I have one last kiss?"

"You don't have to ask, Lia."

Tangling my fingers in his shirt, I yank him toward me. The kiss, which I expected to be sweet, is out of control from the moment our lips meet. We're grabbing at one another as if this is the last time we'll get to touch. Who knows, maybe it is. He reaches down, grabbing my thighs and presses me toward the wall.

I stumble until my back meets the concrete. Once I do, he presses me up against it and moves in between the space I've made there. Desperate, I grasp at his shoulders and hold on tightly. Before I know it, we've unbuttoned his pants, and he's moved the gusset of my panties aside. Pressing his length into me, I groan as he settles home.

"God help me, Lia. We shouldn't be doing this right now, but I need you. Before I go out here and risk my life, I need to have you one more time."

"Yes, Tris. One more time. Mark me, own me, and take me. Please."

He does exactly as I've asked. Thrusting in and pulling out, hitting every piece of my flesh. Burying his face in my neck, he sucks, nipping, marking me as I've asked him to do. It'll have to tide me over until the next time I see him.

Tristan groans as he comes deep inside me. In my mind, I pray that he's leaving a piece of himself there. I'm decimated as he pulls away from me. There won't be any cuddling this time. We won't get to lounge in the afterglow of lovemaking. Instead, he's going to have to leave.

"I'm sorry." He speaks quietly as he walks over to a row of lockers. "I wish I could stay here with you."

"I wish you could too." I'm quiet as I stare at him, watching as he reaches into one of the lockers and pulls out what I recognize as a uniform for the Haldonia army.

It's a reminder that this isn't some sort of video game where we're practicing for what will happen if we're invaded. This is reality. The type of one none of us ever thought we'd be living in. He takes off his clothes, piece by piece, and changes from the King of Haldonia into a fighter. One that appears strong and fierce, the type of man who won't let anyone harm his wife or his country.

When he's almost done, he steps in front of me. "I don't want to do this, Lia. Never in my life did I think I would have to fight for Haldonia. When I went into the army, it was because I had a duty, as does every eighteen-year-old in this country. It was never with the thought we'd have to fight against someone who wanted to take our freedom away. I don't know how to process any of this." He swallows roughly.

And there is no time. The second he leaves here, he's going to be expected to know all the answers to every question. He's going to have to keep the forces ready and willing to fight. If we stumble and trip, then Crona could take the castle and the country. It's as simple and as difficult as that. Complicated and terrifying. None of us thought we'd have to live in this situation, and I don't know how to process this. All I want to do is have my husband wrap his arms around me and tell me that everything is going to be okay. I want him to come home to me every night and assure me that we're going to make it.

But we don't live in a time of certainties. Right now, we have to leave it up to chance and prayer.

"Let me help you," I whisper, reaching up to straighten his tie. Using my hands, I brush off his shoulders and then run them down his chest. His heart is thumping beneath my palm. "Are you nervous?"

He grunts, standing up straighter. "I can be honest with you without worrying that you'll use it against me. So I'll do that."

My heart breaks for him. He's had to deal with so much since he's taken the helm of Haldonia. So much he shouldn't have had to. I'd love to take all his stress and pressure he's under, shape it into a ball, and throw it out into the ocean. "I will always be the person you can come to. The one who understands you without you having to explain it to me, Tris. I'm your shelter in this storm. If you don't want to talk about it, I'll support you in that too."

"No, I need to say it. I'm absolutely terrified that I'll not be able to lead this country to the other side of this invasion. What will that mean for the people? Will they trust me if I don't? Will they blame me?"

His distrust of himself is the worst part about any of this. "They will love you because you're taking control. You're trying to lead, not hiding when that would be easier. You're a great man, Tristan, and no one expects you to have all the answers right now. I just need you to be safe. Please come home to me."

He jerks my chin so that we're looking deeply into each other's eyes. "You are what will give me the motivation to survive every single day. Knowing that you're here waiting for me is what I need. Visualizing the family we're going to have in the future? That's going to keep me fighting. I love you, Lia."

With tears streaming down my face, I tuck my head into his chest. "I love you, too."

And he eventually lets me go. I watch as he leaves, a piece of my heart going with him.

CHAPTER 17
TRISTAN

TWO DAYS LATER

Parker and I are in our tent, where we spend a good portion of our time. Even though it's a couple pieces of canvas, it's the safest place I can be.

"Are we making any headway?" I ask Parker, taking a drag off a cigarette. I haven't smoked since I was a teenager, but desperate times call for desperate measures. There's been nothing else that can stop the tremble of my hands.

"Not yet, but we've stopped their advancement on the eastern side. Right now, we're going to have to be satisfied with that. The first step will be to stop the advancement, and once we do that, then we can fight back. Your general will be in within the next few minutes."

"Thanks. I'll be waiting."

Parker nods and leaves. Although he ducks out of the tent, I know he won't go far. I haven't been able to speak to Lia since I hit the battlefield, but earlier today, I was given an encrypted phone. With everything I have, I hope that I'm able to send her a message she's able to receive.

> T: I hope you're receiving this, L.

I hesitate to use her real name, but I'm confident she'll know it's me since I call her Lia. Almost immediately, a text is returned.

> L: I miss you, T. Is this you?

> T: I wish we were at the weekend house having fish and chips on the beach.

She should know it's me based on what I've said. I'm trying to tell her it's me without revealing too much. The worst thing would be if I accidentally let the enemy know who she is and where she's being kept safe. It bothers me, because I can't be with her. There's no way I can make sure she's safe physically, because I'm here, and I can't be in two places at once.

> L: You have no idea how much I wish that too. It's not the same here without you. Are you safe?

> T: Safety is relative. It's never guaranteed, but I will always strive to come home to you.

My throat squeezes as I think about my wife there by herself. More than anything, I wish I could be there with her. My memories go back to the perfect couple of weeks we were able to just be a newlywed couple. What if this experience changes me in a way I'm not able to come back from? What if I'm hurt to the point I'm eating out of a straw, or I no longer have all my limbs? These are the thoughts that keep rolling through my head.

> L: That's all I can ask. Is there anything I can do for you? Anything we can send to you?

> T: All I need for you to do is keep loving me. To be waiting for me when I'm able to get away and keep thinking about us.

L: I will always love you. There's nothing that's going to make me stop.

T: What if I have to make choices that aren't popular and don't align with who we have been as people? I'm scared to death I'm not going to be the same person when I come out of this, and you aren't going to love me.

L: I'm behind you a hundred and ten percent. Just know I'm here at home praying for you and holding the home together. I'm trying to come up with an idea to do for the people of Haldonia. I'm not sure what yet, but I'm going to keep on.

My heart could burst out of my chest. I love her. She's the best person who could've been appointed my queen. If I had picked someone, it would've been her. I know that with everything inside my body.

T: I love you. Be safe.

L: You too.

"King Tristan, do you have a moment?" It's the general of the Haldonia army.

"I always have a moment for you. Please let me know what's happening and what our plans are moving forward."

He has a seat next to me so that we can look at the map he's spreading out in front of us. "We're planning on moving from the eastern edge and pushing them back."

Nodding, I listen to him as he explains to me what he plans on doing. "Are you planning on starting now?" I question, taking another drag off my cigarette.

"Yes, sir, we are."

Turning to Parker, I raise my eyebrows. "I want to be out there. You know I can fly."

"Your Majesty, you being out here on the battlefield is dangerous enough. We can't have you up in the air."

He stops just short of saying the only reason I'm here is for optics, and that pisses me off, because if I was doing that, I wouldn't be out here on the battlefield. I'd be somewhere safe all the time, giving my directions to how I want others to fight this war. That's not me. I've been on the front lines since we were invaded. "Fuck off, Parker. With all due respect, I've been here the entire time. I've fired guns when I've needed to. Let me do what I've been trained to do."

He sighs heavily. "Tristan, I'd have to go up with you."

"That's fine with me."

He swallows roughly. "It's not with me."

"Oh my god, Parker. Are you scared of flying?"

"Not exactly flying, but heights aren't my friend."

There's never been anything that this man has been afraid of that I'm aware of. "While I'm sorry that you're afraid of heights, it's where I feel comfortable. It's where I can make a difference."

He wants to argue. I can tell by the twitching in his jaw. We've worked together long enough that I know when he's annoyed. At the same time, he won't tell me no unless it's a threat to national security, and he knows I'm good at flying. When I was serving, I was one of the best pilots in the military.

"Okay," he sighs. "If you want to go up, then that's what we'll do."

I turn to the general. "Call and get a plane for me. We'll be in the air within the next hour."

This is where I'm at home. Back when I was piloting every day, I was less stressed, had more patience, and was able to see the beauty in all the land around us. In the cockpit, I check all my instruments and listen as the plan for today's operation is repeated.

"Are you ready, Majesty?" Everyone else had cooler call signs than me, and it always made me jealous.

"Yes, we're ready."

In front of me, the air traffic controller is standing, giving me directions. Everything has been so loud since the invasion happened. All the time there's this buzzing in my brain, causing my ears to hurt. All that noise? It's gone right now. I'm laser focused in and thankful I have a job to do that I can visually notice the impact of. When I get the okay to taxi down the runway, I speak to Parker.

"Are you okay? We're about to take off."

"You do what you need to do, Majesty. I'll be good back here. I don't plan on puking or passing out."

A small smile spreads across my face. It's rare to have a reason to do so these days, but Parker and my wife can usually bring me some measure of joy, even in the darkest moments. "We'll see about that."

My focus is on the jet as we take off, and I radio in our coordinates, verifying what I'm supposed to hit. We're flying to our target, just off the coast of Haldonia. Part of me wonders if Amelia will be able to see what's happening from where she is. Maybe I could do a fly-by, but she'd have no idea I'm up in the jet.

It takes longer than I thought it would for us to get to our target. In the air, I'm flanked by three other planes. "Targets are acquired."

Below us, I can see a row of aircraft carriers off our coast, presumably coming around and going to surprise us with another sneak attack. Little do they know we're the ones who are going to surprise them.

Once I get over them and target lock, I speak calmly into the mask. "Permission to fire. Target is locked."

"Permission granted. Fire upon."

With a flick of my thumb, I make the decision to drop a bomb on this group of carriers and finally feel as if I'm doing something that's going to make a difference. Hopefully after this, Haldonia is able to make advances in this nightmare.

In my mind, all I can think is fuck around and find out. They may have thought we'd lie back and let them crush us, but that's not me, that's not my country, and that's not my people.

We'll fight for it all and not stop until we get it.

CHAPTER 18
AMELIA

THREE WEEKS LATER

I never thought I would be away from Tristan like this. Especially not when we got married. Remembering back to that day, I'm reminded of the person I was, standing at the front of the church. She was unsure of herself, not at all confident in whether or not she'd be able to deal with the pressures of a monarchy. What she wasn't prepared for was keeping up with her husband via an encrypted phone.

Since we got married, this is the first time we've spent apart. Not going to bed with him every night and waking up next to him has filled me with an anxiety I'd never imagined. Every minute of every day, I'm worried that he won't come back to me. It's manifested in me losing a few clumps of hair and not eating like I should.

I'm living for the correspondence through that phone, but there's been none today, and that worries me more than anything else has. Since we got the phone, we've kept in contact. Not constant, but enough for me to know he's okay.

My mood matches the rain pouring down outside. It's promising the birth of a new season, and I'm trying to take comfort in that. No matter what happens with Crona, a new day will dawn. Doesn't matter if myself or Tristan are even here. God has promised that the sun will come up tomorrow. It's hard to remember that belief when the sky around us appears so gray.

"Your Majesty."

My head shoots up as I hear the voice of a man I haven't heard in weeks. Parker. My stomach drops to my feet. There's only one reason he would be here. "Is Tristan okay?" I wait for him to tell me, my heart beating out of my chest. Immediately, the fact I haven't heard from him hits me right in the fucking solar plexus and almost pushes me off my feet with the force of it. "Please tell me he's okay," I beg, my voice watery and shaky. I don't recognize it, or the person this fear makes me.

He nods, and then from behind him is the best sight I've seen in weeks.

My husband.

He's a little battered and bruised, his hair is longer than normal, the beard on his face grown in. He looks older and even wiser. It's as if everything he's been through is written across his face and coming across his eyes like a TV show. Only this isn't make-believe. This is real life, and if I lose him, it's not as if he can be revived. I'm glued to the ground for a long moment, but then it's as if my brain and body come back online. I take off at a run, before jumping up. His arms come around me, holding on strongly.

Tristan's gotten stronger since he's left. His body has been honed by what I imagine are hard days and nights. When I pull back, I map his face, memorizing every inch of the man I love, the one I gave myself to. I've missed him, and I'm scared to death this is going to be the last time we see each other. His eyes are tracing my face.

"You look exhausted," I whisper as I track the dark circles marring his otherwise perfect skin.

"I am," he whispers back. "But I wanted to see you. I had to see you. It'd been too long. I wasn't sure if I'd be able to take the rest of this campaign without seeing you."

I nod, trying to hold back the tears. His lips meet mine, and as he sets the pace for the kiss, the tears come falling down, just like the rain outside. It's washing away all the fears and doubts. "I love you." The words are quiet as he pulls away. "How long do I have you for?" This is what our lives have become. We're forced to sneak important moments in between military operations and threats to our safety.

"A day, maybe a little more. I needed some time with you, and a good night's sleep. Parker encouraged me to come home."

Reaching up, I wrap my arms around his neck, holding on for dear life. "I'm glad he did. I've missed you." When I pull away, I run my hands up and down his chest, checking him to make sure he's safe. That no one has harmed him in any way. Tears spring to my eyes again, and my throat tightens as I think about how happy I am he's here. But at the same time, I realize there's been a tremendous sacrifice by others. There are plenty of women and men who won't ever see their spouses again. For now, I'm lucky mine has been able to come back home to me.

Our foreheads meet between us. He rolls his against mine, inhaling deeply, as if he can't get enough of my scent. I can't get enough of his either. My fingers are grabbing at him, making sure he's right here in front of me, and this isn't an illusion. His deep voice speaks. "I want you right now, but I'm dirty. Can I take a shower first?"

I don't want to let him go, not even for a minute. It's too long, considering how few hours we get to spend together. "Can I join you?"

He closes his eyes. His lashes brush against my skin in feather-light touches. "Are you sure? I'm not the man who left here a few weeks ago."

"And I'm not the woman you left." I set my jaw, refusing to take less than what I want. We might not have years left, not like I imagined when we got married. "I can handle it."

His calloused hand comes up to cup my cheek. "I love you, Lia. You're the reason I do this."

"And you're the reason I keep sane, knowing you're out there. I can't imagine my life without you, but I also can't imagine what it's like for you."

A guttural sound escapes his throat. "It's hell."

Tilting my head up, I put a small kiss to his lips. "Then let me take you to heaven, even if it's just for a little while."

Finally, he gives in with a sigh. We separate, but it's as if he can't make his feet move. I get it. It's been difficult to put one foot in front of the other while he's been gone. Reaching down, I grab his hand and lead us to the bathroom. When we get there, I have him sit down on the closed toilet before I walk over to the shower.

He drops his chin to his chest. That's when I allow myself to take in my husband. His body looks absolutely defeated. Pulling my lip in between my teeth, I bite down hard enough to draw blood, to keep myself from gasping or responding to how much I hurt for him. Reaching in, I turn the shower on, adjusting the water to where I hope it's warm, but not hot.

Tristan still hasn't acknowledged what I've done when it's gotten warm enough, and there's steam filling the room. He's so stuck within his own head, I'm not sure I'll be able to get him out. Walking over to him, I shed my clothes, and it isn't until I unhook the bra and let it fall that he gives me his gaze.

"You're beautiful," he whispers, almost reverently.

I've never been at a loss for words with him, but I don't know what to say. How can I? I don't know what he's been through, what he's seen, and he won't tell me. Anytime I've been able to talk to him, he deflects, which is what I would do, too.

Gripping his shirt in my fingers, I slowly slip it over his head and off his body. It takes everything I have not to have a reaction when I get a good look at his chest. He's lost weight, and there are scratches, along with bruises, along his ribs. "Tris, what happened?"

Grabbing my hand, he entwines our fingers and brings it up to his mouth, kissing where they are connected together. "War happened, Lia. It's not pretty. None of it is. There are moments where it's not as bad as others, but none of it is good. Even the outcome isn't celebrated, because we know what it cost to get there. I've lost a portion of my men. Haldonia is ruined in places. It will take years to rebuild." He sniffs. Those eyes of his are tortured, and I would do anything to take away his pain. "They hit the royal cemetery, and with it they destroyed my mother's grave. For that, I will have Calder's head on a silver platter. He will wish he never met me."

This is a side of Tristan I've never seen before. War brings out the best and worst in humanity. It also opens up a side of people they don't know they have. This is what it appears to have done to Tristan. He's hungry for revenge, and in my experience, revenge gets people killed. Terrified doesn't begin to cover it. "I love you." I trace his features with the tips of my fingers. "I love you so much."

"I love you too," he answers.

For the first time since he came home, it doesn't feel as if those words are on autopilot. The emotion behind them is there.

"Let me take care of you. It'll soothe a part of me that's been complete chaos since you left."

Those eyes are full of pain from the things he's seen, definitely done, and what he has to do when he goes back. "Let me see the beauty and good in the world, Lia. Show me so that my heart and soul don't shrivel up and die."

Those words kill me, and I vow to myself that no matter what I have to do, I'll show him that I'm here. The rest of us are here, and we need him to continue to fight. I'll give him the courage to go back out and win the battle for our nation.

CHAPTER 19
TRISTAN

When I'm out of my clothing and in the shower, I tilt my head back, allowing the water to flow over my body. It's washing away everything.

The terror, the pain, the hurt, but at the same time, the dreams I have for my country. For my family. For our future. Amelia takes the reprieve to grab a bar of soap and lather it along the muscles that make up my body now before taking the showerhead off and making sure I'm completely rinsed.

Then she winks, and I'm wholly unprepared for what happens next.

This woman can bring me to my knees, especially when she's dropping to hers in front of me. I need this more than I realized. To know that someone loves me, that they're waiting for my return. It's so hard to feel any kind of emotion out in the field right now. Not when we're taking fire every day and night. All we can do is try to survive.

But survival is fleeting, and being thankful only lasts for so long.

There comes a time when I have to have something tangible to attach myself to. Such as my fingers in her dark hair as she kneels in front of me. When she lifts her eyes to mine, and grabs the root of my cock, rubbing it against the seam of her lips.

"Take it, Lia. Give me something to live for. Something to look forward to."

She doesn't say anything, instead she opens her mouth and takes my cock down her throat. Her moan fills the shower and sets my body on fire.

"Son of a bitch, Lia. Take me down farther. You do this so good."

Tightening my fingers in her hair, I use my grip to move her back and forth on my length, my toes curling against the floor of the shower. She doesn't say anything. She just grips my cock harder, moving her hand up and down as her lips follow.

I've lost weight in the last few months, so it's easy for me to reach down, grasp her elbows, and pull her up onto her knees. When she's there, I release her hair, smooth my hands down her neck, shoulders, and then down to her breasts. Cupping my hands around the fullness, I flatten my palms, worrying the tightened nipples as I move them back and forth.

Closing my eyes, I tilt my head back against the wall of the shower, swallowing roughly as I give myself over to my wife. So many nights I've thought about being with her while I've been out in the field. That's not completely the truth. Not only am I thinking about how hot her mouth is, I'm thinking about what our life could be like in a few years. Hopefully, we'll have children, we'll still be together, and our country will be at peace. "Lia, I don't want to come down your throat." I push those words out through my tight neck. "I want to come inside you, want to make sure my line continues."

She pulls back, eyes lift back to mine. "Tristan." Her tongue comes out to lick her lips, and she moves her face out of the way of the water pouring down. "Are you saying you want to have a baby?"

"Yeah." I nod, digging my fingers back into her hair. "I want to know when I leave here that if something happens to me out there, it won't be the end of my life. More than anything, I want you to contact me in a few weeks, and I want you to tell me that you're pregnant. That what we're going to do over the next couple of days is going to make a baby. Then I want to see your stomach grow with the seed I planted, your tits swelling with the nourishing liquid that will feed our son."

She has tears in her eyes and a smirk spread across her face. "What if it's a daughter?"

"God help the man who decides to love her."

Getting up, she drops my cock, entwining her arms around my neck. "I want that too. More than I ever have. Give me something to live for while Haldonia is going through this dark time. I love you, Tris. Now fuck me like you've never fucked me before. Let's make a baby."

She doesn't have to tell me twice. Reaching down, I grab her around her thighs and lift her up onto my waist. "Wrap your legs around me and hang on." Amelia is a good girl. She always does as I ask. Together we make our way to the bedroom. Once there, I toss her down and then stand over her. My gaze runs from the top of her head to the bottom of her feet, committing to memory how amazingly beautiful my wife is. It isn't as if I didn't know before, but the last time I looked at her feels as if it were a lifetime ago. Reaching up, I place my hand over my heart. "Everything I do after there, I do for you."

"I know." She reaches forward, grabbing my arms. "Now take care of me like I've been dreaming for you to."

Leaning forward onto the bed, I let it take my weight as I press against her. She makes room for me in between her thighs, and I settle there as if it's home. Her slickness shines against the lips of her pussy as I fall back onto my knees and run a finger along her heat before slipping it into the wetness.

"Oh Tristan, that feels good."

Hooded eyes stare back at me, and I'm a bit of a sadist lately. Smirking, I look down at her. "Have you been using your fingers while I've been gone? They're a poor substitute."

"That and toys," she admits, heat blossoming on the apples of her cheeks.

Using another finger, I spread her apart, turning my wrist so that I'm hooking them up into her pussy. Using a "come here" motion, I stroke inside, letting my thumb rest against her clit. It doesn't take long for her hips to move against me. "What kind of toys?" My voice is wrecked. It sounds like I've swallowed a ton of gravel on the morning of a bender. "Are they as good as I am?"

She shakes her head, reaching behind her to grip the sheets in between her fingers. "Nothing is as good as you."

"You're fuckin' right about that, wife. No one can fuck you the way I do. No one knows what you like, like me."

Her eyes close as she thrashes against the mattress, her hips lifting, her thighs slipping further apart. It's lewd the way she's spread for me, like she's the leading actress in my personal porno. My cock is bobbing out in front of us, and I'm torn between the need to reach down and give it a few strokes and the want to see her fly apart in front of me. Her eyes fly to mine, and she must notice where I'm looking, because she loosens her grip on the sheets and brings one hand down to my hard length. When her small hand wraps around it, I throw my head back, groaning loudly.

"Yes, baby, stroke that fucker. Break me apart."

I need to feel it. The little death that an orgasm brings so that I know I'm alive. There have been so many times in the last few months when I wasn't sure whether I was alive or if I was just surviving. Being with Lia makes all of that crystal clear in my mind. Without her? I'm surviving. I'm not truly alive if she's not next to me. The spark of her, the way her body smells when it's aroused, the smile on her face, those are necessary for me to thrive. With her, I'm living the life I've always been supposed to live.

"You're so hard, so strong, fucking long, Tristan. I don't remember you ever being this hard." She muses as she moves her hand along my hardness.

It's because I haven't. Not being around her like I normally have has magnified every feeling I have for her—including sexual need. I've never been so horny while being with the object of my desire. My ass is tight as I try to stop the pleasure coursing through my body, my nipples are lifted toward the sky because of how tight my skin is, and my balls are drawn up under my cock.

When I can't take it any longer, I move her hand aside, hold the base of my dick, and press into her. Dropping forward, I take her tight nipple into my mouth, working my tongue against it as I thrust into her body. We both groan deeply as I seat myself home.

"This is what I missed," she hisses, digging her fingers into my shoulder blades.

I palm the side of her breast, holding it still while I use my mouth to worry her nipple against my tongue, and then take a taste with a nip of my teeth. When I'm not sure I can take holding still any longer, I swing my hips, withdrawing from her body.

Her pussy holds on tightly, not wanting to let me go. I yank my mouth from her breast, blowing hot air on the wet skin. "You've gotta let me move, baby. Let me fuck you. I'll make it good for both of us."

She reaches forward, grabbing my chin and leveling our gazes together. "Don't take it easy on me, Tris. I want it rough, hard, however you need it, and I want a baby."

Our eyes meet, and I see the rest of our life there. The child we're going to have, what Haldonia looks like in the next few years, and what we hope to achieve. "Hold on then, I'm about to wreck us both."

With those words, I withdraw completely and then drive home. It could be thirty minutes, could be hours later, but I'm still fucking her. Sweat drips off my shoulders and down into my face. My arms are shaking, knees are raw, and my cock is hurting because I need to come so badly. But I know when I do, then the first part of our time together is over. I have to face going back out into the field, and I'm just not sure I can. Not when I'm buried so deep inside her.

Amelia's mouth opens and her eyes roll back in her head as I thrust harder. "Tris, I'm gonna come, need to come."

I do too. Reaching between us, I put my thumb against her clit and grind into her. "Shatter for me, Amelia. I'll put you back together." It's a promise built against an oath of keeping her safe.

She nods, digging her fingers into my neck as she grinds with abandonment, reaching for the elusive end to this game we're playing. Just as her body tightens, I let go, coming hard against her, my cock jerking three, four, and then a fifth and final time. It destroys me, and I send up a little prayer that I'll leave her something to live for if it turns out that I can't make it back to her next time.

CHAPTER 20
AMELIA

His long lashes are fluttering against his smooth skin. I would give anything to know what he's dreaming, what he's reliving. It doesn't look good, not with the way his head is thrashing against the luxurious material of our sheets. Reaching out, I run my fingers along his forehead. It's hot and wet with sweat. His eyes pop open as if he's on high alert, and he sits straight up in the bed.

"It's okay, Tris, it's me."

"Are you in trouble? Is someone here to hurt us?"

The fact that he's worried about being safe in our home is terrifying. "We're fine. You're fine. Things are going to be okay."

He grabs hold of my wrist, his fingers tightening in a circle around it. "I don't know that, Lia. I've always assumed if you be the good, then you'll get it back, but look at what's happening around us. So many good people who had absolutely nothing to do with any of this are gone, and for what end? A piece of land that was never theirs to begin with?"

My heart hurts for him. He's been on the leading edge of this shit show since the beginning. From the night we were fired upon, he's worked day and night to ensure the people of his country are safe. Unfortunately, that hasn't always been the case, and won't always be, because of the world we live in. "We don't always know the end. We just have to pray that the end will justify the means."

He swallows roughly before glancing up at me. "It's hell, Lia. Every single night. It's hell. Hearing the screams, the cries of my men. Those who are in pain, both mental and physical. The ones who are missing their family members and their homes. I can't bring them back, and it kills me."

He tightens his hands into fists and beats against the bed.

"Stop." I reach out, putting my hands over his to halt it. "If you have aggression, take it out on me."

"You don't know what you're asking." His voice is full of gravel and deeper than I've ever heard. "You don't understand what I'm capable of anymore."

My heart is pounding so loudly, I'm not sure how he can't hear it. It's a reverberation in my ears so strong that I want to reach up and cover them. Even when I know all it's going to do is magnify the sound. "I trust you," I whisper. "With everything I am, I trust you. I can take whatever it is you need or want to give me. Believe it or not, I want to be the person that you come to with those feelings. Use me and abuse me if that's what you need."

He makes a noise in the back of his throat, and that's when he attacks me, pushing me backward onto the bed and covering my body with his. "I don't want to hurt you."

"You could never hurt me," I assure him, reaching up to cup his cheek against my palm. "But if you need it rough, then I do too. Don't be afraid to give me what you need."

He growls like I've never heard, spreads my legs apart and dives deep into my core. He takes me in a way I never thought he'd be able to. Gone is the man who was more worried about my pleasure, and in his place is a man on a mission. What mission? I'm unsure, but I feel it as he thrusts in and then pulls back out with an intensity I'm not used to.

Hooking my legs around his waist, he holds on tight to my ass cheeks. "God, Tristan, this is so different than how you normally are."

He buries his mouth in my neck as he lifts one hand and brings it down hard against my flesh. It makes a loud crack that causes me to groan loudly. "Feel good, baby?" he questions, pulling back and slapping my flesh again.

"Yes, do it more."

I never realized I would like a little walk on the wild side, but with my husband, I'm willing to try anything. Part of it may be because we haven't seen each other in a while, and the other part may be because he seems more virile than he ever has.

"Tristan," I whisper, hoping he can hear me over the sounds of our bodies slapping together.

He bites at my jawline, bringing his hands up to mine, entwining our fingers and pressing them up above my head. "What?"

"Make me pregnant." My voice breaks as I say these words.

He stops, his eyes meeting mine. "Do you know what you're saying?"

"Yes." I tighten my legs around his waist. "If you don't come back to me, I want a reminder of you. Give me your baby."

An absolutely feral sound erupts from his throat as he presses his knees into the bed and rides me hard. We're straining against one another, both wanting the other to come. "You want me to fuck you and make you pregnant? Give you my seed?"

He's never spoken like this before. It's so fucking hot. "Yes, I'm here, I want it all. Come for me, Tristan. Come inside me."

Opening my thighs wider, I undulate into him, taking every inch of his body. Sweat breaks out across both of our bodies. We slip and slide against one another. "You want it?" he asks, his voice full of passion and deep with gravel. "You want me to give you my child?"

"Yes, more than anything, I want that."

He releases my hand, slapping his palm next to my head. "I wanna give that to you," he grunts, his teeth gritted and his hips swinging into mine.

"Then do it." I reach up, pressing my hand to his chest. "You've gotta come."

"I'm trying," he pants.

The hand pressing to his chest travels up, and I wrap my fingers around his throat, applying pressure. "I need you, Tristan. Come for me."

"Tighter," he pushes out between those gritted teeth.

I do as he asks, and he loses control. His rhythm is gone, and all of a sudden his body seizes up, his head thrown back as he comes deep inside me. When I feel his heat, I'm right there with him, dragging my fingers down his chest, hoping that I mark him so deeply he'll remember my love while we're apart.

CHAPTER 21
TRISTAN

This is the hardest part of the situation we're in. Leaving her, knowing that she won't be able to come with me. Who knows when I'm going to be able to see her again? My arms go around her, holding on tightly, so much that I lift her off the ground. Burying my face into her neck, I whisper, "I love you. I'm going to miss the hell out of you."

She sniffles, and the noise tears at my heart. When she pulls away, her eyes are red with the tears she's cried. Her voice cracks as she speaks to me. "Be sure and come back to me, Tris. I don't know what I'd do without you."

I want to promise her I will, but there aren't any certainties in this life we're living. "I'll do my best. That's what I'm going to promise. I've never broken a promise to you before, and I don't plan on doing it now." The words catch in the tightening of my throat.

This time it's a wounded noise, and it strikes me right in the middle of my chest. "I know you're the type of man not to make promise you can't keep. I get why you won't say the words."

Pulling back, I frame her face with my hands. Running my eyes over her face, I commit this moment to memory, to go along with the one of the first time I saw her. There are certain things I've thought about constantly when I've been out there. Situations we've been in where she's told me she loves me, important moments in our lives.

When I'm at my lowest, I think back to our wedding day and the first time she told me she loved me. The ones that weren't so important too, like the day we spent riding my bike. They're all the small minutiae of what make up our lives together, and I'm terrified I'm not going to have the years with her I planned on. "You're right, and this season we're in, I'm completely unsure of what I can deliver. Just know that I love you, I'll do whatever it takes to get back to you, and if I don't make it? It'll be your name as the last word on my lips."

This time, she sobs, burying her head in my chest, and holds on tightly with her arms around my waist. "I love you, Tris. I'll love you until I'm dead, and then further, until we reach heaven. I'm never giving up on you, Tris. They'll have to drag me away from you. Promise me that you'll have someone tell me immediately if something happens to you."

"That I can promise." Dropping my lips to the top of her head, I give her a kiss. I've got to leave her, and this is the hardest thing I've ever done. "I love you, Lia, but I have to go."

Tightening her arms around my waist, she holds on for dear life. "Everything in my body tells me that I shouldn't let you go. That I'll regret it. That I won't be back or be the man I am right now. There's no way to know the future, and I hope I'm back here as soon as possible. However, I also know what everyone else doesn't. We're starting to lose this war, and it's going to take a lot for us to turn this around. We've lost part of the lead we had, and I'm scared we aren't going to get it back."

There's a potential, always one, that we won't win this. If that's the case, I have to keep Lia and me safe. They will come for us, and they won't make any concessions, especially not for her. They'll use her to try and get to me. If there's a chance they can get information from me, they'll use her to get it.

"Are you ready, sir?" It's Parker, gently interrupting us in the quiet way he always has. "The helicopter has landed, and it's not good for it to be sitting out in the open."

He doesn't have to say it makes not only it, but us a target. "I'll be right there."

Glancing down at Amelia, I give her a smile. If asked, I'm not sure how I do it, but all I can think of is this. I don't want her last memory of me to be one full of dread and sadness. If she has to think about the last moment she saw me, I want it to be a smile.

"I can't let you go." She tightens her hold on me.

"You have to." I reach behind me, unhooking her fingers and removing her arms from my waist. "There are people expecting me, and there are places I need to be. Please don't make this harder than it has to be, Lia. I love you."

"I love you, too." She sobs.

When she finally drops her arms, I sneak out of the room, and wipe at the tears under my eyes. Inhaling deeply, I fill my lungs with the air I need and turn my attention to Parker. "Brief me. What's happened while I've been gone."

"We took back the north, and we're making strides to the east. Once we get that, we can initiate the final attack."

Me coming home was part of a bigger plan. While the Calders were watching me to see what I was going to do, our forces launched coordinated attacks on the two weakest points of entry. "Numbers?"

Parker doesn't even have to look at anything. He remembers it. "We lost eight, and they lost a total of two hundred. It was bloody and savage, but for them, not us. They got a taste of their own medicine."

I guess it makes me human to be proud that we unleashed domination upon them, considering the way they surprised us with an attack we weren't prepared for in any way. Since then, we've been fighting for our lives, and it increasingly felt like we weren't making headway.

"Let's get back to the field."

As much as I haven't wanted to, I know that it's where my place is.

CHAPTER 22
AMELIA

I'm beating my hand against the window as I watch Tristan and Parker jog across the yard toward the helicopter. The rain is pouring down, matching the way my stomach is jumbled up and down. Below us, the ocean is angry and crashing against the rocks. It reminds me of every feeling I have watching him leave. My heart is flying away from me, and I feel as if there's a dark cloud hanging over us. It's as if this is the last time I'm going to see him.

Sliding down, I pull my legs underneath me. Great sobs that rack my body are escaping my throat, tears are streaming down my face. I can't stop as I suck in deep breaths of air, trying to keep myself from hyperventilating, but it's not working.

"He's going to be okay." That's Shannon. She's holding on to me tightly as we rock back and forth on the floor. I'm still amazed at her since she proved how she can handle a weapon.

"How do you know? Since we've been invaded, there's a dark cloud hanging over us, one we can't seem to shake. I'm terrified that this is the last time I'll ever see him. What if he doesn't come back?" I gasp, trying not to hyperventilate further. My stomach is aching, saliva gathering in my mouth as I try to keep from throwing up.

"There are no guarantees in life, Amelia. I learned that at a young age, and while it's annoying to hear over and over, it's the truth. You might drop dead with a heart attack the moment you walk out of this room. Tristan could die doing something mundane, like driving to the next parliament meeting. What we have to do is take the moments that mean something—the kisses, the words, the little touches—all of those and hold them close to our hearts." She runs her hands along my hair, bringing me to her side, cradling me as if I'm a baby. "Remember all the things that you love about him. The little things he does, the crinkling of his eyes, the smile he has just for you."

While I know she's right, and it's about the sum amount of everything and not the big moments, I can't shake the feelings I'm having. They're big and all-consuming, competing with the happiness I know I should have for the life we've lived before the invasion. "I know that you're right, but it's going to take me a while to get used to it. It's not easy being away from him. Quickly, he became my best friend and the person I look for in those crowded rooms. How do I survive without him?"

She grabs my hands in hers. "You put one foot in front of the other, and you force yourself to move. Whether that means becoming the face of this or not. I think the people of Haldonia would love to see you. It would give you something to do other than sit here and wonder how it's going on the front lines. It's a win-win."

Rolling it around in my head, I think about all the other people in our country. How are they handling this, how much are they missing their loved ones? No one knows because there's been a social media blackout. Towers were hit at the beginning of the invasion. "Are there enough towers back up for me to be able to do this?"

Shannon nods. "It's something Parker has been working on, too. He knows how important it is for all of us to stay connected."

"All right, if we're able to transmit, then let's do it."

She holds up a hand. "I'll go make sure we can, and you make yourself ready."

Pulling my bottom lip in between my teeth, I chew at the lip. "What is your opinion on what I should wear? I don't want them to think I'm standing around in formal dresses while they're struggling to put food on the table. I'm struggling too."

Here are those tears again. I've never been so emotional in my life.

"Then that's what you tell them, and you wear what you're comfortable in." Shannon smiles. "I'll be right here in the background. Get yourself together, and I'll verify we're able to do what we want."

Nodding, I watch her leave, and I let myself have a bit of a breakdown. I fall apart for the woman I was, the life we thought we were going to live together, and the loss of all the dreams we had for the first year of our marriage. Closing my eyes, I think about the ones who have decades-long marriages, and they've had to say goodbye to their spouses, for kids having birthdays without their parents.

Walking over to my closet, I flip through everything that's hanging. Nothing speaks to me, and I'm pulled over to Tristan's side of the closet. There are a lot of things over here I can't wear, but my gaze and heart are drawn to one of his favorite sweaters. It's gray and warm, he's worn it a lot, and every time I see it, I think of him.

One of the first dates we went out on after we got married was to get dinner, and he wore this sweater. I can close my eyes and remember that night. He'd purchased a flower from a street vendor and handed it to me as if he were handing me the world.

What I wouldn't give to go back to those times. Taking off the T-shirt I'm wearing, I slip this one over my head and then walk over to the mirror. Running a brush through my hair and putting on the slightest amount of makeup is all I do.

Shannon comes in. "We're a go. Do you want to do a live feed, or do you want to record it? We can do either."

Nerves wreck my gut as I take a seat in front of one of the walls, painted a deeply masculine color. As I'm waiting for Shannon and my personal bodyguard, Monica, to tell me I can go ahead and get started, I twirl my wedding and engagement rings on my finger. It's a nervous habit I've picked up while waiting for Tristan to come home. It makes me feel closer to him.

"We're ready when you are." Shannon offers me an encouraging smile.

Swallowing hard, I give her one back and then motion for them to turn the phone on. "Good evening, people of Haldonia. It's been a while, hasn't it?" I smile, although I can feel it shaking. "I'm sure all of us are doing our best to make it through the situation we've been handed. Now that we can broadcast things again, you can expect me here every day at this time." I take a moment to center myself and get my breath back. "More than anything, I want you to know I'm praying for all the families who have lost a loved one, for those of you who've had your lives irrevocably changed by the actions of the Calder family. What I can promise you is Haldonia and the king will fight with every single breath in our bodies, and we won't stop until we have every centimeter of land back.

"Speaking from my heart, I want those of you who have loved ones in the field to know I sympathize with you, and I'm praying for their safe return. I know that gut-wrenching dread you get every time you hear the phone ring, then when you realize it isn't someone informing you your loved one is dead, you break down into tears. I know how hard it's been to be on rationing of food—I'm right there with you, and I'm missing my husband as well." I stop for a second, licking my suddenly dry lips. "I promise you that I'm right here with you. Anything we're asking you to do, I'm doing as well." Reaching down, I pull out the sweater, surprised at the tears that once again pool in my eyes. "Including wearing my husband's clothes because all I want to do is smell his cologne and feel his presence next to me. This was a spur-of-the-moment thing. I wasn't sure I could do it, but I will, every day, and I hope to see you tuning in. Haldonia, you have all my love."

I wait until Monica and Shannon let me know they've turned off the feed, and then I collapse slightly into myself. That adrenaline crash is crazy. "Did I do okay?"

Shannon grins. "You did amazing, and judging by the comments on social media, your fellow country members feel as if you did too. Look at this."

She shoves her phone in front of my face, and that's when I see it. Thousands of comments.

TaylorLoverHaldonia: It was so good to see Queen Amelia's face after so long. I was worried they'd hurt her, and that's why she hadn't made a statement or appearance.

HarryT: @TaylorLoverHaldonia Same, I've been looking for this since the beginning. Thank God she was able to come through for us. I always knew she would. Her and Tristan are relationship goals. The rest of the world is watching us, and these two are the epitome of a couple standing together and strong in the face of adversaries.

Emotional doesn't even begin to describe how I'm feeling. This whole situation has taken such a toll on every single one of us. "I'm thankful most of them took it for what it was. There are probably a lot of people who don't think it's enough. Truthfully, I don't think it is either, but it's the one thing I can do."

Shannon gives me a soft smile before smirking. "And we love a queen that puts others in front of herself."

The laugh bubbles up in my throat. "Thank you. I love you, Shan."

"Love you too."

CHAPTER 23
TRISTAN

It's loud where we are. Thick smoke hangs in the air, the acrid scent invades my nose. There are bombs going off in the distance. Gunfire is closer than I'd like for it to be, but if there's one thing I've learned, it's that if I hear all of it, I don't have to worry as much. That means there aren't people sneaking up on us. They're being loud about what they're doing and not trying to come in under the cover of night.

"Did you hear?" Parker looks over at me, a smile spread across his face. It's rare. I haven't seen one from him in a long time. Even spending time with Shannon while I was visiting Lia hasn't been enough to bring him joy.

"The gunshots in the background? They're white noise for me at this point." I grumble as I look at the information coming through in real time, making sure that our forces are doing what we need them to do.

"No." He shakes his head, amazement showing in his eyes. "What Amelia did."

Immediately I'm worried. Anything having to do with her worries me. What if the enemy is threatening her? "Can you show me?"

He shuffles around, grabbing his phone out of his pocket before putting it in front of my face. "Look what she did. She did an amazing job. I'm not sure if you two talked about this or not, but it's a great idea."

I have no clue what he's going to show me, but I'm wholly unprepared for what I see. It's her face, stoic and strong, looking out toward the camera as if she has no fear in the world. With my heart pounding in my ears, I listen to what she's saying, and the pride I feel is enough to strangle me. When she and I met, I could see this within her, but I wasn't sure I'd ever see it.

"How are the responses?" It will kill me if the people of our country aren't supporting her as much as she's supporting them.

"They're amazing. We couldn't have planned this better if we tried. Most everyone is speaking out in support, thankful that she's becoming the face of the nation."

Tears pool in my eyes as I think about my wife being the amazing person she is, going above and beyond for us. I'll never understand how I got so fucking lucky. When I was told that my marriage was arranged, I didn't think I'd have love. In fact, I'd relegated myself to not having it. I thought I'd live my life being halfway satisfied and still wanting something to make me whole. Never did I think I'd have everything I wanted with this woman.

There aren't a lot of people who can say they've fallen in love with their arranged marriages, but here I am, completely and totally in love with mine. "God, I miss her. We've got to get this over with so I can get back to her. So we can get back to our normal lives. Fuck them." I tighten my jaw, my fingers curling into my palms. "Fuck that country for what they've done to us. For them being so jealous of what we have and trying to take our natural resources. Killing people who live here and not even caring. How long are we going to fuck around?" Then I realize I'm the one who has to end this.

"You want to get done with this, you know what we have to do."

Parker's right. I do know what we have to do, but I'm terrified of making the wrong decision. It only takes one for the support I have to go the other way. "I'm still undecided."

"Only you can make the decision."

"It's true." I reach into my pants pocket, the ones I've changed back into after I got back from visiting Amelia. My nerves are shot, and the only thing I've been able to do in order to calm them down, is smoke a cigarette or two. I used to do it when I was a teenager but stopped because there was such an outcry with the tabloids. However, desperate times call for desperate measures. Putting it in my mouth, I hold it while I cup my hand around the flame of my lighter. "In one hand, I'm thinking about how we'll appear to the rest of the world. In the other, I'm hoping to get this over with and go back home. I can end this with one call, Parker, but at what cost?"

His mouth firms into a line. Both of us know what I'm saying and what it means. "You're not the type of person to use other people to make your sacrifices, Tristan. I don't know if you could live with yourself."

That's the biggest issue. I'm not sure if I could live with myself either. This isn't who I am, and it wasn't what I thought I was going to have to do when I took the oath to be king. "That's what it's going to come down to. What can I live with? Will I be able to look at myself in the mirror the morning after?"

"Most heads of state would give this up to a vote, Tristan. Do you think that's what you should do?"

I've thought of it, more than I care to admit. For long hours out here on the field, while I hear people screaming, when I hold my gun and fire shots. It's on my fucking mind. But I can't seem to pull the trigger on the actual plan. It's been presented to me more than once. I just don't want to have to answer to the people of my country if I'm wrong. It's a lot of pressure, and I'm terrified I'm going to make the wrong decision.

"I can hear you thinking over here, Tristan."

"I refuse to put it up to a vote. If it's the wrong decision, I want to be able to take the responsibility for it. Protecting the members of my cabinet are of utmost priority. Just because I'm scared to decide doesn't mean I should push it off on someone else, Parker."

"What's going to make you force the decision?"

Good question. I haven't gotten there yet. "I'm not sure, but I'll know when I do." My stomach is aching as I think about what we've been forced to do. "I want to go out on the battlefield."

"Your Majesty, it's not recommended. Not after the attack we were just under."

It pisses me off that he tries to protect me in this way. There isn't a way for me to ignore what we've been going through. I need to see everything that's happening out there. If I stay here in the tent being sheltered, then I'll never be respected or understand enough to grow into the leader that this country needs. "I'm going, Park. Either you come with me, or you don't."

He's not about to let me go out there unprotected by him, so he nods, and together we head out onto the battlefield. We get into an armored truck and head the twenty miles to where the last fight was taking place.

When I get out, I can smell it, the stench of death. The thick smoke hangs in the air like fog along the ocean during the summer. I wish I could transport back there right now, but it isn't an option. My eyes scan the number of bodies that are lying there. Knowing that many of these men won't be able to go home breaks my heart. It hurts me in ways I can't articulate.

As we come upon another group of soldiers, one of them moans, reaching out to me. "Your Majesty."

Without thought to my own safety, I kneel down to the ground and take his hand in mine. "Save your breath. They'll be here to help you in a few moments." What I don't say is that I'm not sure he has that long. "Let me know what I can do to help you."

He licks split lips, marked white with the dryness of his skin. "Make sure my family knows I did this for them, and I'm not sorry I died on the battlefield."

"You're not going to die." If I could make him live by force of will, I would do it.

He chuckles, but it turns into a hack. "Please save me."

Beside him, someone else moans, moving his head back and forth against the grass. "Your Majesty," the other person whispers out from what sounds like a gravel-laced throat. "Can you help save me? I'm not ready to die."

Goddamn, this is harder than I ever imagined it would be. They're looking to me to save them, and I can't. I'm not God. I can't take away their pain or save them from the inevitable. "I won't lie to you. There's nothing I can do to help you. What I can do is stay with you."

"I would be honored," one of them says.

"Hey, are you with me?" I press against the other one's shoulder. "Stay with me."

His eyes pop open, but there's nothing in them. It's as if he's looking out into nothing. The life and any emotions are gone.

"Please tell my wife I love her," he whispers, his breath rattling as he takes his last one.

"I will." My throat closes in upon itself. Turning to the other man, I hold his hand tightly. "What can I do for you?"

"My wife. My kids. Tell them…" His breath is coming in short, shallow gasps. "Tell them that I did this for our country, so that they could be safe and free. Let them know I didn't do this in vain."

"They will know. I'll make sure they're taken care of for the rest of their lives."

And in that moment, he's gone. Along with the patience I've had for Crona.

CHAPTER 24
AMELIA

The days are long and growing longer as Tristan stays out in the field. I thought for sure he would be home by now, and this would be behind us. I've been trying to keep busy, writing down my feelings about what's happening in Haldonia. It's helping me to work through some of the issues I'm facing.

Shannon comes running in, her hand over her mouth. Her eyes are wide. "Have you heard the news?"

"No..." Immediately my body is cold as I think about what might cause her to hurry into the room like this. There's not much that will get either of us completely worked up. We've learned over the past several weeks to not get messed up by things that don't matter in the long term. If not, we were going to drive ourselves crazy.

She hurries over, grasping my hands in hers. "I just got the notification, and I don't know much more than what I'm about to tell you."

"Is he alive?" I cut her off. "Just tell me if Tristan's alive." Swallowing roughly, I rub my wedding ring with my thumb and send up a prayer that my husband is okay. My eyes are on hers, going back and forth, needing her to tell me something, anything.

"He's alive," she whispers. "But I think he's been hurt. The message is hard to decipher."

Her hands are shaking as she thrusts the phone she uses with Parker toward me. It's encrypted, like the one I have. My eyes travel over what's typed out, but she's right. It's really hard to decipher. It seems as if half of it is written in a language I don't speak. "I need to know what all of this means, Shannon." My nerves are shot, so unlike the calm, collected person I've been since I took the title of queen. "There's no way I'm going to be able to give the address to the nation without knowing what's going on. Please, can we figure it out?"

Neither one of us knows what to do. There's a loud knock at the door, and we immediately glance at one another. There aren't many who know where we are, as far as we're aware. We've had few visitors besides Tristan and Parker. Monica's been around, but a lot of the time we don't see her.

"Let me answer the door." She grabs a knife from the kitchen.

"What are you going to do with that? If they get close enough, they can turn that knife on you. Why don't you hand it to me, and if they get it, and we need it, I'll take care of it."

Her jaw drops. "I can't let you do that."

Wrapping my arm around her shoulder, I turn her toward the door. "It doesn't matter who does it, Shan. You can't go grab your gun. They'll be able to see it if you're holding it. We have to know what's happening out there, and just maybe the person on the other side of that door can tell us. Give me the goddamn knife."

Her eyes widen. My face flames with embarrassment. It's not often I lose my cool like this. In fact, I can't remember it happening before this very moment. Grabbing the knife out of her hand, I turn her toward the door. "Open it."

She hurries over and cautiously opens the door.

When I get a good look at who's standing outside, I gasp. "I know her. She was my detail earlier in the year. At the ball, before all this happened."

"At your service, ma'am. I've been sent to make sure you're okay. Now that King Tristan has been injured, your security is stepping up."

I'm torn between believing her and being worried that she's lying to me. What if someone knows she's the one person I would trust blindly? Only because I want to know what's happening with my husband. A long-ago conversation with Parker comes back from some-where within my brain.

"What's going to happen if I need to know that someone is safe? How do I know that?" I tilt my head to the side as Parker continues to make notes about what my security detail will look like once we're married.

He stops what he's doing and looks me straight in the eyes. "Listen to this, and commit it to your memory bank."

"I will."

"Anyone who is on your detail will have to say this phrase in the heat of any kind of dangerous situation, where you might be in danger. If they don't say this, then you absolutely do not trust them, no matter who they are."

The weight of how much this means is heavy on my shoulders. "What phrase is it?"

I'm back here in the entryway of our home, with the kitchen to my back. "You know I need you to say a phrase for me. If you don't, I'll make you wish you never showed up here." I grip the knife in my fingers.

I stand still, trying to hide my fear. It wraps around me tightly. I'm scared she's here to ruin everything. I keep my body straight and my lips firm, hoping she knows not to mess with me.

Her gaze softens. "Queen Amelia, I am here to cook your breakfast."

Tears fill my eyes. My heart pounds so hard that I might collapse, but I'm relieved. Shannon and I aren't alone anymore. Someone is here to help and protect us. That's the phrase I've been taught to request. Suddenly, I fall to the floor, shaking with fear strangling my throat and tears clogging it. Both of them kneel beside me. I look up at her and ask, "Tell me he's alive, please. I need Tristan to be alive. What do you know?"

She quickly shuts the door and helps me up. She looks at me like a mother would at a frantic child. "Amelia, if I'm allowed to call you that?" she asks.

I nod, giving her my permission. "This isn't normal. These are desperate times, and we need friends. Yes, call me Amelia, please."

"He's been injured, and that's why I'm here," she explains. "There's a threat to you, too. There are people around who have been keeping you safe, but starting now, you're under my care. I will protect you. Do you understand?"

I nod slowly, still thinking about Tristan. "But what happened to him? Please tell me, I'm dying."

She swallows hard and grabs my hand, leading me to the kitchen island. "Have a seat," she says gently, "and we'll talk."

This is exactly what I wanted, and I hope like hell I'm ready for it.

CHAPTER 25
TRISTAN

TWELVE HOURS EARLIER

It's still quiet. Almost too much, as if something is coming for us. I've learned to question it all since this war started. If it's too loud, if it's too quiet, if it's not loud enough, if it's not quiet enough. I've become almost crazy in my thoughts. It's enough to drive a person over the edge, and the only thing I've been hanging onto is Parker being here with me.

It's annoying because I used to be okay with anything. I could handle the moments where I didn't have to hear others speak. The car I had? I'd drive it way over the speed limit just because I could. Over a hundred miles an hour did nothing to my stomach. It was how I proved to myself I was alive. I could handle fireworks and things of that nature, but now I'm not sure what I'll be able to deal with once this is over. It's changed me significantly.

There's a fear that Amelia won't love me anymore, that I'm not the man she married, because I'm not. Maybe she won't be able to handle the man I've become. There are things I've seen. There are things I've done. Things I'm never going to be able to forget. Can she accept it? I don't know. We'll have to see. I'm as terrified about that as I am about how this war will end.

Parker lies next to me a few feet over at the entrance of the tent we're in. I've never been in a tent before this. I've never done a lot of things before this. Not to say I didn't train. In the military I did, but I never once believed I'd have to do it when it counted. It was very much one of those, just in case I need it, type of things.

But those were the before times. Before the Calders decided to invade. Before they took every ounce of security and safety I felt and turned it into something that I will never be able to forget.

He grunts as he rolls over, bringing his coat tighter around his body, and looks over at me. "I know I'm the one who shouldn't be giving you thoughts that don't make sense, but does this feel weird to you?" he asks. "It's been a while since we've had quiet, especially for this extended amount of time. I'm worried. I'm scared," he whispers. "We haven't defeated them yet. This feels like the calm before the storm, as if they're planning on doing damage when we least expect it."

Those are the exact thoughts that have been rolling around in my mind for the last hour and a half. Instead of being able to relax because there's not a ton of noise around us, it's got me more on edge. "Me too."

I don't know what any of it means. I'm not sure what they're planning on doing, and I am terrified, absolutely terrified. These are the moments when I wish Amelia was here, when all I want is for her to wrap her arms around me, to give me her hand, a simple smile. It would all make it better. Her careful and stoic strength is desperately needed.

While we've been able to talk to each other through text, it's made me miss her more since I left our visit. Relying on those texts to make my days isn't healthy, but I give into the need.

T: Love you. I hope to see you soon.

Waiting for her to reply, I rub at the wedding ring on my hand and think back to our wedding day. Think back to how happy I was, how many plans I had, what the future held for us. It was so bright, unlike the darkness of this moment, the dank tent we're in.

There was happiness, and now there's none.

"Now I get it," Parker says as he looks over at me. "There's definitely something going down. Last week, there was some chatter on a few of the lines we listened to, and I didn't want to tell you about it, but maybe I should now."

Immediately, anger courses through my body. "Goddamn it, Parker. You're supposed to tell me when anything happens. This isn't the type of situation where you spare my feelings or spare my ink or spare my fear. This is scary, but we're all facing this. We must know when there's a threat, if there's a threat. Why would you do that?"

He sighs heavily. "I'm supposed to protect you, Tristan. I've been protecting you for years. With this, I can't seem to do anything right. It's as if I don't know what the fuck is happening. They're under the radar, and I don't understand how."

I hear what he's saying. I don't understand it either. There have been so many times where we should have known what they were going to do, and we didn't. Now that we're on the offensive, we've made headway, but I am worried—desperately worried—that we're going to lose it as quickly as we got it.

Swallowing roughly, I look over at him. "I'm scared. For the country, for my life, for my wife, for you, for Shannon, for everyone. But right now is not the time for you to hold things back from me for the sake of what you think is my sanity. I have people to protect. There must be truth in everything you tell me. Promise me—promise me, Parker—don't hold back."

He nods slowly. "I promise." And with that, he starts to say more.

His words are cut off by a loud cracking in the distance and what appears to be the detonating of a bomb not far from us. We both get up off our cots and look at one another. My hands are shaking as I get up from the cot, my stomach feeling as if a bunch of nerves are firing at different intervals.

We haven't gotten undressed because it's not something we do on the battlefield. Sleeping in our clothes has become second nature and a way of life. Like a synchronized unit, we're putting our weapons on when someone cuts through the tent. The flash of a long blade is closer than I would like, and my life as I know it flashes before my eyes.

"Let's go," Parker yells. "Get out of here. I'm right behind you."

I take off at a run and don't look back.

As we race into the dead of night, the horizon lights up like it's a freaking Sunday on crack with mortar shells exploding around us. I can see Parker as if he's standing in broad daylight, looking at me. There are men—men I've come to know well—lying dead around us, and I am absolutely gutted by what is happening. I don't know how to stop it. I don't know how to put a band-aid on it, and I'm not sure what my next steps are.

Parker grabs me by the sleeve of my shirt and yanks me toward him. "My king, now is the time where you must protect yourself. We have got to get out of here."

I understand the tone of his voice. It says there's nothing for me to do, and I don't have time to mess around. With a nod, I put the shield up on my face so I can see what's happening but don't react. We're running—running toward an armored vehicle that's waiting for us. I keep my eyes locked on it, knowing that this is freedom, that this is how I'll get back to my wife, this is how I'll still run this country.

When I'm ten feet away, there's a loud, loud bang. It knocks me flat on my back, off my feet, and the world goes black.

CHAPTER 26
AMELIA

I'm on the edge of my seat as I wait to hear what she has to say. It's as if I'm on the precipice of a cliff, trying to keep myself from tumbling over. I'm breathing heavily, my heart pounding. There have been a million things rolling through my mind. Is he barely hurt? Is it life-changing? Is he on the cusp of death? It's all crowding into my chest, making it feel as if an elephant is sitting there. I want to rip off the clothes I'm wearing and take a long deep breath, but I can't. I can't until I find out how Tristan is doing.

In the short amount of time we've been together, he's become my life. He's become everything I want, everything I need, and I'm terrified to live this life without him. There isn't one without him. Although he was forced upon me, I've come to count on him. He makes my life better, my heart happy, and brings a smile to my face.

She taps her nails against the marble of the counter before looking over at me. "With everything happening, I believe I need to introduce myself to you officially."

I think back, all the interactions the two of us have had together. I don't know her name. I've never called her anything other than my detail. I'm ashamed of myself. That's not how I was raised, to treat someone who protects me as hired help. I try to remember why I've never asked her. Maybe it was because I didn't want to get too close and not have someone I've thought of as a friend go away.

"You're right." I smile. "I'm so sorry I've never asked you before. What is your name? If you're going to be here with us, we need to know that. We don't call people 'details' when they're a part of our everyday family. And trust me, that's how I feel about anyone who works with us daily. You're a part of the family."

She pulls her bottom lip between her teeth. I can tell she wants to say something about that, but she's struggling. I keep speaking, hoping to bring her out of her shell. "Everyone will tell you that as queen, you're not supposed to have favorites. You're not supposed to bring them further into the fold of your life, but I can't help it. That's not who I am. That's not who I want other people to know me as, which is why I'm doing these daily transmissions to the people. We all need this right now. If I'm not reaching out, holding my hand for others to grasp onto, they're going to feel lonely, as if the leaders of this country do not care, and that's just not the case. So if Tristan can't do it, I'm going to do it."

"My name...my name is...Maddie. Matilda, really, but everyone calls me Maddie."

"Matilda." I grin. "I loved that story as a kid."

She pushes her eyes upward to the heavens. "So did my mom, which is why I was named that. It's a pleasure to meet you, Amelia."

Her eyes are warm, and that's what I'm counting on more than anything. I need a friend, not just a protector. Only having Shannon around has been hard. I like her, but at the same time, being with the same person for an extended period is almost suffocating. "You too."

I reach out my hand for her. It's a firm handshake. I don't expect less, but it's important that we meet each other in the middle. "Now please tell me about Tristan."

She licks her lips and pulls a phone up from her pocket, scrolling up. "I have a video for you, but first, so you're not shocked by what he looks like, I want to explain what happened."

My stomach clenches. Why would I be shocked at what he looks like? What has he been through? After all of this, is he gonna be the same man he was before? How could he? My fingers wring with worry as I wait to hear what she has to say.

"They were attacked," she begins slowly and carefully. "It was a surprise, and they weren't prepared. Someone broke into their encampment first and then the tent that Tristan and Parker were in. They managed to get out."

Shannon reaches out, grabbing my hand with hers. There's a but to what she's saying. Neither of us wants to hear that anything is wrong with the men we love, but it's hard. It's hard to know they are somewhere and we're nowhere near them. "They took off running to where there was an armored vehicle waiting for them. However, right before they could get on, there was an explosion near where they were, and both of them were knocked backward."

She stops for a second, looking at us. More than likely making sure we can take whatever else she's going to tell us.

"They have a lot of cuts on their faces because of debris, but they're okay. I want to reiterate—they are okay. There are some more injuries besides the cuts. There are some cracked ribs, but nothing that's going to be lifelong and nothing that you're going to have to worry about."

I breathe a sigh of relief. None of this is going to interrupt our lives together. Not that it was make it or break it, but that's been one of my biggest fears. I've been worried if I was faced with the decision to take care of him the rest of our lives, I wouldn't be strong enough.

"They are okay, but they're pissed about what happened. I don't know a whole lot about it because we're on a need-to-know basis, but I do know that there are plans being moved forward, which is why I'm here with you. There have been threats made, and that is why I'm here."

Shannon rolls her lips together. "Can you be honest with us? Does this mean that we are going to make a big..." Shannon stops, then starts again. "Does this mean that we're going to do what I know neither of them want to do? Are we going to bomb the other country? Are the Calders going down?"

Maddie doesn't say anything, but the look on her face tells us everything we need to know. I gasp, covering my mouth with my hand. That must have been a really hard decision for Tristan to make. I know it's one he didn't want to.

"Amelia, you need to prepare yourself. None of us know what the outcome of this will be. However, we know that making this decision is dangerous. It puts us right back in the crosshairs of the Calders. Which means you are the one who is in danger. Tristan is heavily protected on the battlefield. You? You're a sitting duck."

"Right back in the crosshairs?" I question if we've ever left them. We didn't do anything to start this in the first place. They wanted our little country. They thought we wouldn't fight, and here we are, fighting with everything we have. "And don't worry about me. I can handle myself. If they want to come for me, they can. I have no doubt my husband has put enough protection in place that they won't be able to get to me."

I'm debating on whether I want to keep speaking. How much does Maddie know? There's no way I want to spill Tristan's secrets, but it's imperative she understand where I'm coming from.

"Tristan is not going to let this go. He loves the people too much. He loves himself too much. There's so much pride. His mother died here. She's buried here. He's not giving it up easily, as he shouldn't."

My mind drifts to the beautiful man who is my husband. I can only imagine how this is tearing him apart. No matter what he tries to portray in public, he is so empathetic and has such a great heart that this must be killing him. Finally, I ask. "How can I support him?" I firm my bottom lip and look at her as if I don't have a fear in the world, yet I am scared to death. She runs her hands through her hair.

"I need you to make another video and address tonight."

I'm confused. "I've already been doing that."

"Yes." She pulls her bottom lip between her teeth, "but you need to announce that you agree with everything Tristan is doing. That you are behind him one hundred percent, and you feel as if there's no other way after what happened today."

I swallow roughly. This is hard. It's not going to be easy, and I'm not sure if this country will ever forgive me if this goes bad. However, I know that I have to stand behind Tristan. He wouldn't do this if he felt like there was another option, and he's been close to death more times than I care to count.

This one could have ended him, and now we've got to end this.

We didn't start it, but we're damn sure going to finish it.

CHAPTER 27
TRISTAN

My whole body aches in ways I never imagined. Then again, I've never been so close to a bomb going off, it's never knocked me off my feet.

I'm tired but wired. My hands are shaking with the adrenaline dump after what's happened to Parker and me over the last few hours. When I knew it was my turn to take over this monarchy, I never imagined any of this. Never thought I would be the person making these decisions. Never imagined someone would come after us like this. After all, to my knowledge, they hadn't the entire time I've been alive, but my dad could have kept things from me. I'm learning he more than likely did.

We're sitting in a hospital room, doctors standing in front of us as they look over our bodies. I'm aching, and I know there's a chance I broke some ribs, but all I want is to talk to Parker. This attempt on my life—because that's what it is—has pissed me the fuck off. "I'm ready to bury them." I grimace as the doctor wraps my ribs. "They wanted me dead, and they were going to get it any way they could. Didn't matter who they hurt."

The doctor speaks. "You didn't break anything, Your Majesty, but you're going to be feeling it for a while. I'll be giving you some pain medicine."

"No." I stop him. "I don't want it. My mind needs to be clear for the decisions I have to make."

He looks as if he wants to argue. "Let me give you something, please."

"Over the counter will be fine. It's important I'm clear when I go before Parliament and tell them what I want to do. When all this is over, I'll spend the time to rest that I need. I promise."

"It goes against everything I believe and all the oaths I took, but if that's what you want, that's what I'll do."

I set my jaw and nod. Opening my hand and thrusting it toward him, I wait until he puts a few Tylenol in my palm. What I wouldn't give for a pain pill right now, but if I'm going to possibly decimate another country, I have to be cognizant of it. Dry swallowing isn't my favorite thing to do, but sometimes it's a necessity.

Parker looks at me, tilting his head to the side. He walks slowly over to where I'm sitting, grimacing as he wraps his hand around his side. "Are you sure you don't want to hold a vote?"

I shake my head. There's no way I can take a vote and protect my cabinet at the same time. "No. Just in case this goes bad, I do not want other members of the Parliament to be able to say that they voted for this. I want them to have a lot of plausible deniability. And then we'll see if I get overthrown if it goes bad."

My stomach hurts. I'm not sure what I should actually be thinking. How nervous I should be. But I am inconsolable. All I can think about is if this goes wrong. What is going to happen to our country? What will happen to Amelia? Chances are, if I've made the wrong decision, I'm not going to make it through this night or the next few days. And it terrifies me to leave her.

But my hand has been forced by people who do not care for this country, who do not care for me, and who don't give a shit about human life. All of that has been blatantly pushed to the forefront. So now I'm making a decision that's difficult, that no one wants to make, and that I will stand by until the end of time.

Now that we've been cleared, we leave the hospital and hop into an armored car. It's unnerving riding in traffic. It's as if we're on display and unsafe. Before, I never felt unsafe, even in the middle of the war.

My hands are shaking, and I'm sweating, but I refuse to say anything to Parker.

It seems like the longest ride, but eventually we pull into the underground parking lot.

Within minutes, we're out of the SUV and heading to the conference room. Once we get there, I see that others have been called in.

Glancing around the room at the few trusted people who have been allowed to stand with, to sit with me, I take it all in. Notice members of Parliament that I've appointed, that my father appointed before me. I see the worry in their eyes. The way they don't know if this is right. I take that and push it into myself and realize that this is something that's going to change the rest of our lives. But if I don't make this decision, we're not going to have lives to live.

And that is the scariest part of all.

I look over to the head of our military force and give him a nod.

"Send the bombs."

And we'll deal with the fallout later.

I watch on screens that relay live camera feed with my arms folded across my chest. We aren't bombing the entire country—just the military and the royal family. And I brace myself for the pushback and possible retaliation.

But I refuse to sit back and do nothing anymore.

They wanted us, and now they got it.

CHAPTER 28
AMELIA

I've never been so nervous and proud at the same time. Tristan has made one of the hardest decisions anyone has ever had to make in this monarchy. Which is why I want to support him in the best way I can, and since I've gotten a following with the broadcasts, this is how I'm going to do it. My lips are dry, so I reach over and grab the bottle of water sitting next to me.

I try to ignore the shaking of my hand as I bring the bottle to my mouth. A large gulp wets my throat and gives me the kick in the ass I need.

Shannon is standing behind the cell phone, waiting to give me my cue. "You're going to do great," she says. "I'm sure the residents of Haldonia are waiting to hear from you. It's like you've become their best friend through all of this. You're the person they can count on every single day. I know you don't see it, but they count on you. The little bit they get on social media, they talk about how they look forward to your daily addresses. They know at three in the afternoon, they can connect to the feed, and there you are."

That's so much pressure. More than I ever anticipated. When I started having these talks every day, I never expected for them to be the battle cry of a country, but that's what they appear to be. This one is the most important I have ever given, and I have to make it count.

Shannon makes the motion to let me know that I am being broadcast out to the citizens of Haldonia, and I take a moment to stare at them even though I can't see them. I want them to know that I understand everything that's happened here. It's nothing to take lightly. We have changed the trajectory of our history, and it's important that we acknowledge it.

Licking my lips, I start. "Good evening, people of Haldonia. I've made it a habit of coming to you every afternoon and giving you an update on what's going on. By now, you will have heard that Haldonia has attacked our neighbors. This was not unprovoked. King Tristan himself was targeted over the past few days, and late last night, early this morning, he was injured by Crona forces."

Here is the part I want to reiterate. It's important for the people to know that Tristan made this decision because he felt as if it were the right one.

"What King Tristan decided to do was not taken lightly, ever. This was his decision and his decision alone. I stand by it. He chose to aim missiles at targets that were military and members of the Calder family. He purposely decided to stay away from parts where civilians would be, as he does not want to harm them, unlike the Calder family who bombed a market here three days ago. There were fifteen civilian deaths. Fifteen! And then they have the gall to come after your king? After my husband? They're never going to stop unless we stop them."

I take a moment to center myself and breathe deeply in order to keep my emotions in check. Knowing Tristan could've been easily killed still bothers me. There are times when I catch myself thinking about what my life would be like without him. It doesn't feel good, and the one thing I've learned is I never want to experience it. He means more to me than anyone else in my life.

He is my life.

The present, the future, and everything in between. So I need the members of our country to know we must trust him. He has nothing but our best interests at heart.

"I hope you realize that this was not an easy decision for Tristan.

He never wanted violence, but his hand was forced. I hope that you all stand by him, understand the difficult decisions he's had to make, and agree with what he ultimately decided to do. He will take responsibility for any of the blowback. I know him. I love him. He is a good man—a great man—who has high integrity, and if anyone has to answer for what he's done, it will be him."

Inhaling deeply, I place the onus on Tristan to answer any questions that citizens of our country may have. It's not easy to make these decisions, but it's imperative we listen to any concern that anyone may have. At the same time, I want everyone to know we have the same end game. As long as we're strong together, no one is going to stop us.

"I hope you all join me in a prayer tonight for the people that we've lost and for the decisions we've had forced upon us by someone else." I tuck a piece of hair behind my ear and lick my dry lips. "We pray that this is the end, that we can go on and live our lives peacefully, and that we don't have to deal with this again. No one deserves it. No one wanted it except for the people who started this. All we want is for it to end, and hopefully this is where it does."

It's my greatest hope, and I know that Tristan believes the same. All we want is to live in peace, like we were before.

"We will rebuild no matter how long it takes. Haldonia will come out on top, and we will be stronger than we ever were. My love is with you all tonight, and I hope that you're all hugging your loved ones. I pray I'll be able to hug mine soon, and while we won't be back to normal ever again after the things we've seen and what we've had to do, we will be united with love, empathy, and the desire to live our lives the way we want to."

Tears have pooled in my eyes, and while I've been reluctant to show my emotions previously, now is the time for me to drop that rigid hold I have on myself, and let the people of this country see it all. They start out silent, just streaming and gathering at the edge of my cheeks. My chin collecting them until they spill over, like raindrops on the edge of a bucket. Once they get there, and spill over onto my neck, the sobs start in earnest.

I'm not even sure what I'm crying for. Is it because I miss my husband? I'm scared because I don't know what's going to happen in the future, or just because of the emotion dump I'm experiencing. Although we haven't been in this situation for years like some countries, it's still been stressful. The stress, the not knowing what's going to happen, and not having my husband by my side has been the hardest thing I've ever been through.

Shannon hands me a tissue from where she's standing, and it makes me cry harder. My face falls into my hands, along with the tissue. She does something she's never done before. She steps out from behind the camera and comes over to where I sit, wrapping her arms around me.

"Are you okay?" she whispers, rubbing up and down my back.

"Yeah," I whisper back. "Just give me a few seconds."

The sobs work through me, my breath hitching as I try to calm myself down enough to continue to speak. It takes a few times for me to not feel shaky. She walks back behind the camera. I close my eyes and wipe at the tears before opening them and staring back at the camera. "I love you all. I'm praying for you all, and we will come out of this together. We are strong, and we've got this."

I nod slightly at Shannon to let her know to cut the feed. When she tells me that she has, I ball in upon myself, letting out great sobs full of anxiousness and desperation. The only thing I want right now is to hug my husband, but because of this situation we've been forced into, I can't.

Steadying my chin, I give her a sad smile. "I don't know about you, but I need to go to bed."

It's early, but I need peace and quiet. All I want to do is look out the window, toward the ocean, and let it soothe my soul. I trudge up the stairs knowing I'm going to bed alone and realize just how much I fucking hate it.

CHAPTER 29
TRISTAN

The live feed from Crona is as if I'm watching a video game, and this isn't real life. Did they do this when they dropped the bombs on us? Did they watch the people outside in the markets as they ran for their lives? Did they high-five and grin with glee as we scrambled to figure out what the hell was happening?

I'm so far away from that right now that I'm about to be sick. I hate that I had to make this decision. This kills me me—watching members of their cabinet and military—running for their lives. However, each of those people made a decision regarding who they would follow. No one forced them into it. Crona isn't like Haldonia, where members are required to do military service. Their military is one hundred percent voluntary. These men and women? They decided, with their own brains and hearts, knowing what the leader of their country was like. Those members of the cabinet? They ran, knowing the kind of man they would serve under.

I don't want to watch this any longer than I have to. "When do you think we should know something concrete?" I ask the head of our military.

He glances over at me, his nose flaring as he inhales. "Soon. We've taken out ninety-five percent of their base, which means they don't have ammunition or vehicles with which to deliver a counterattack on us. This blitz has done exactly what we wanted it to. It's over, King Tristan. We won't allow them to have enough ammunition to put together any kind of answer to what we've done."

Accomplishment makes my chest expand with pride. It shouldn't. I shouldn't be so proud of what I've just done, but I want this over. I want to go home to my wife. I want to sleep with her every night, talk to her about having children, live the life we were living before this hand was forced upon us.

Guilt threatens to suffocate me, as I realize there are people who have fought on both sides who will no longer have these options. I can't say I enjoyed having to make this decision, because I didn't. If there could've been any other way for me to protect my people, I would've. We were backed against the wall, and there was no other decision for me to make. If we want to live freely and in peace, then this was what I had to do.

More than anything, I want the country of Haldonia to prosper and thrive, to not have to worry that this will happen again. And the only way I will do that is by making a stand such as what we've just done. I'm exhausted, tired of it all. I don't know how leaders of countries do this for years at a time. Maybe I'm not cut out for leading my people. Or maybe I need to cut myself a break and focus on what I'm able to do.

Either way, all I know is I can't wait to go home, sleep in my own bed, hold my wife, and not think about any of this again. Parker taps my shoulder. "Let's go get cleaned up and get a good night's rest. We'll know more once the sun comes up."

The sun coming up is what worries me. People will see the destruction and the decision I've made. They'll know I'm the one who did it. And if there is anyone mad about it, I'm the person they're going to come to. That or they could come to Amelia.

I'm scared to death of her being the target of others because of what I've done. Parker taps his phone. "Did you see Amelia's address? She did good. She's going to make an amazing queen. Her words were poised, deflective, and sure. That's all we ever could have asked for. The emotion she showed proved how she's a leader of the people."

Anger rises in my chest as I think about how she's put herself in the middle of this. How she's made herself a target. "Parker, with all due respect, fuck off. There's nothing that will make me believe that having my wife emotional on a national telecast proves what kind of a leader she is. That's bullshit and disgusting that others want to see her pain. I'm not as patient as I used to be, and if I see people making fun of her, I'm going to fly off the handle, Parker. That includes you."

"I'm not making fun of her." He holds his hands up. "I'm saying how good it was for the people to see her be as emotional as she was. It allows them to know that she cares deeply."

"Why wouldn't she care deeply? This is her country as well as ours. I don't want others to force her to show emotions that she isn't sure she wants to. I'm aware that I'm shooting the messenger, Parker. But I can't stand it. I can't. We've been through too much. You and I know what Crona is going to say about what we've done, and I'll be damned if she gets caught in the middle of this." My chest is pumping up and down as I finish talking to him.

He nods, dipping his chin into his chest. "We both know that, but they don't. They see this as Haldonia being power hungry because of how we have grown in the past few decades."

To the outside world, the Calders could spin this however they want to. It's important the true narrative be exposed, and by us bombing them, putting an end to this, that's what's going to happen. We never wanted to harm them. They have always wanted to hurt us.

But the truth is I'm not sure of any of this, and I won't be until we're told that they've surrendered. Only then, and only after I have a signature and a promise, will I be able to relax and go home.

CHAPTER 30
AMELIA

The sleep that I fitfully fell into after making the declaration to the people is interrupted by gunshots in the distance. Immediately, I shoot straight up in bed, worried about what this means. My heart is pounding, palms are sweating, and the worst-case scenario situations are running through my brain.

Are we under attack here? Have the plans that Tristan had gone sideways? Where is he, and is he safe?

Scrambling from the bed, I grab the cover and wrap it around my shoulders and run to the window, looking out to see if there are forces approaching us. This has been my fear since this started. That the enemy would find me, kidnap me, and use me to get to him. All I could think about was the torture both of us would be put through.

Me physically. Him emotionally.

I didn't realize how much this has been affecting me. My hands shake and my stomach is tumbling as if it's in the ocean below us. Where can I go? What can I do? But as I look outside, I see everyone who lives on the island outside our home. They're holding up guns and firing at the sky. I'm not sure what to make of this. There are a few different scenarios that could be happening, and I'm terrified of most of them.

All I want to do is puke. Nausea is spiking my gag reflex, but I manage to push it down and run toward the door.

"Maddie," I yell. "Shannon, what the fuck is happening?" There are equal parts fear and hope in those words. Still in my pajamas, I dash out of the bedroom and down the stairs. That's where I meet Maddie, Shannon, and a few others I've met before. They're members of Tristan's detail.

"What is everyone doing here? What's happening? Did I miss something?" Scenarios play in my head. Is he somewhere on the battlefield bleeding out? Is my name on his lips? Have they been waiting for me to wake up to give me the bad news? The room is starting to spin, and my hands are tingling. Looking around the room, I'm waiting on someone to be honest with me, to tell me exactly what's happening.

Shannon smiles over at me. Tears in her eyes, but relief spread across her face. "It's over. They surrendered and just signed a peace treaty. Tristan's on his way home, which is why his detail is here—to make sure nothing has been planted around the house or inside it."

I take a deep breath for the first time in a long while, not impeded by the tightness of everything happening around us. The shakes work their way through my body. "Is that why everyone's outside with guns shooting in the air? They're celebratory?"

"Yeah." Maddie grins, shaking her head. "They're celebratory. They really want their queen to come out, but I don't know if it's a good idea with what you're wearing." She glances down at my body, covered by my pajamas.

It only takes me a minute to think. They've seen us all at our worst. All they've ever wanted was a king and queen of the people. They've wanted two people who can understand what their lives are like. Not everyone has the option of deciding on how they're being seen, and it's important to me that I give them every bit of who I am. Which means they want my excitement, the emotional pieces that make us human. Right now I'm so excited that I don't know if I can go upstairs, change, and then come back with the same excitement and honesty I have now. Throwing caution to the wind, I rake my fingers through my hair and pull the blanket tighter around me before walking out onto the front porch.

The people of the town are close and can see me, but they're far enough away that I feel safe. Maddie stands over to the side, as does Shannon. I'm as protected as I can be.

There's a loud burst of applause and greetings yelled as I do. I wave, holding the blanket tightly to me with one hand. I can't hear what they're saying—there are so many things being said at once—but I can feel it: the love, the appreciation, the relief. It's all there, coming to me in a vibe that I can't deny. It brings a huge smile to my face, and I'm grateful for every one of them.

I don't know what to say, so I just blow kisses and yell that I love them and that we will rebuild. They start applauding again, and emotions overwhelm me. I sob, holding my hand up to my mouth. Their feelings come across the yard, and it almost knocks me over. Sharing this moment with these people is everything I imagined it would ever be. They deserve it.

I'm about to turn around and go inside when I get a whiff of it—the cologne that my husband wears. The door opens and loud screams and cheers, louder than anything I've ever heard, erupt. And I know, with everything I have, that the man I've missed so much is home.

I turn around, and there he is—the remnants of battles he's fought on his face—but his eyes are everything I know. They're him. He makes large strides toward me, and that's when I forget the blanket. I let it drop and wrap him in my arms as he wraps his around me.

"You're home," I whisper, those tears falling freely.

"I am, and I'm never leaving you again."

It's the best hug I've ever had in my life—one I'll remember forever—and I'll cherish it close to my heart when I tell our children the story of us.

CHAPTER 31
TRISTAN

There is a lot of work for us to do, but right now, all I want is to reconnect with my wife. Tomorrow will be here, and I can start on rebuilding after I take a day and night to decompress. It's imperative I have this. There's no way I can be a good leader without it.

Letting go of her waist, I pull her to my side, and we present a united front to the people. "Thank you all for coming out to celebrate with us," I start, hoping my voice is clear and strong as I speak to them. "But please keep in mind that celebrating for us is one thing. Those of us who have been harmed, including the people of Crona, are picking up the pieces. We shouldn't celebrate to the detriment of others. At the border, there are residents fleeing, trying to enter Haldonia." I clear my throat. "We will allow them to come into the country as long as they can prove they are fleeing. Please welcome them with open arms. We, as a country, have always been welcoming to those that are seeking asylum. That won't change."

There is another round of applause and more cheering.

"Tomorrow we will work on getting started with rebuilding, but today I'm going to take a moment to spend time with my wife. I missed her, and I don't know about you all, but it's been a few weeks since I've been able to fully relax. I've proclaimed today a national holiday. Spend time with your friends and family. If your home has been damaged by Crona, there are shelters set up all over the quadrants of the country. Tomorrow we begin the hard work"—I grab hold of Amelia's hand—"as we've done everything. Together."

I breathe in deep air that's not filled with the stench of war and death. The smell of the salt and grass washes over me and begins the healing process. One that seemed so distant when I was on the battlefield. Amelia and I wave before turning to go back into the house.

We're surrounded by Parker, Shannon, and Maddie, along with a detail that hasn't left my side since the war started. "Thank you all for your service. Enjoy your day off. I'm releasing all of you." Parker looks as if he wants to argue, but I shake my head. "Nope, you're free to take time off too. I've made sure this can happen. We all deserve it."

When everyone leaves, I'm left with Amelia. It's the first time we've truly been alone, save for a couple of moments since this first started. I pull her into my arms and then tilt my head to the side, kissing her neck. "Would you like to go upstairs?"

"Yes." She grins. "I want nothing more than to spend time with you. God, I've missed you."

"I've missed you too, Lia. Thank you for waiting for me."

"There was never any doubt."

Hours later, we're wrapped up in one another. The way the bed is situated is in a way that we can see the sunset from where we are with the window open.

"Tristan, are you okay?" she questions softly. "I know you've seen a lot, and I can't even begin to imagine what you've dealt with."

My throat tightens as I think about what I should tell her. In the end, I decide I should be honest with her. There's no other way for us to live our lives. "I'm not okay right now. Happy to be here with you? Yes. Relieved that you weren't hurt while all of this was going on? Yes. However, I can't tell you that I've not been affected by what we've done. There are things I'm not sure I'll ever be able to get out of my head."

She runs her nails up and down my chest. "Like what? Let me in to help you."

"One night, I walked through a group of soldiers who were injured. Two of them were dying, and they reached out to me, begging that I help them as their king. I couldn't." I wipe at the tears that are gathering in my eyes. "There was no saving them, not with the way they were hurt. Instead of lying to them, I kneeled and held their hands as they departed the world. At least then they weren't alone. None of that was easy, and I'm not sure I'll ever be able to forget any of it. It's fundamentally changed me."

"Oh, Tristan, I don't know what to say."

I shake my head, holding her closer. "There's nothing you can say. Nothing is going to help other than time and maybe some therapy. We can't take back what was done to us. The only thing we can do is move forward with the best of intentions. We're never going to forget what's happened to us, Lia, but we can overcome it."

She sighs, burrowing her head into my chest. "I believe you. We're still going to have the best life. It just may look different than what we thought it would. All I know is I want to be with you forever."

Closing my eyes, I dig my fingers through her hair. "I had a lot of hopes and dreams when I was on that battlefield, Lia."

"Yeah?" She turns her face toward me and plants a kiss onto my chest. "Tell me about what kept you going out there."

Tangling my fingers, I drag her as close to me as she can be before I tell her. "All I could think about was us having a child, a baby that would be a sign of hope in the times we've gone through. I dreamed of it. A little boy with your smile and my hair. The next generation of the monarchy, conceived among all of this hate and violence. Very clearly, I've seen that he will be the one to settle us all down." I don't tell her that the dream I had was of him connecting us and Crona with a daughter from their family. It sounds insane, but it woke me up from our nightmare. It was the only thing that kept me hanging on when I felt like I was losing it while I was away from her.

She smirks up at me. "I have a feeling that's going to happen for us, Tris. I really do."

CHAPTER 32
PARKER

I'm not comfortable leaving my king without me. From the moment I came out of special forces, my life has been dedicated to Tristan. Over the past few months, I've done nothing but watch over him and worry about what the two of us would be facing.

It's hard to turn that off. Especially when I've been living on the edge for so long. Both of us have been, and it's much needed that we have these moments with the women in our lives. They're the only reason we made it back. I believe that more than anything else. Every time I thought about giving up, I would think about Shannon or having to tell Amelia that I'd let something happen to her husband. I couldn't handle it.

"Parker, come back to me." Shannon's soft voice cuts into my thoughts.

"Sorry, I'm not used to the quiet anymore. It's weird how you get used to so much noise around. At first it was overwhelming, and we spent most of our time overstimulated, but then it became a comfort. When there was noise, we knew that no one would be sneaking up on us."

Shannon sighs, wrapping her arms around me. "That's horrible, Parker. We went through a lot here, but nothing like that."

We're standing in the shower, and I'm trying to wash the last few months off of me. Not only the dirt, but the feelings I've been grappling with for killing other people. Which I did in order to protect Tristan. There were three men that Tristan never knew about.

"Tell me," Shannon begs. "What's going through your head? I want to help you, but I can't do that unless you let me in."

I've never had an issue letting anyone know how I've been feeling, but this experience has changed me. Although special forces prepared me for the situation, it didn't prepare me for the experience. Leaning over and pressing my palm to the wall of the shower, I let the water flow over my shoulders, hoping that it washes away the feeling of despair bearing down on me like a dark cloud. "You sure you want to hear about this?" I turn to look at her.

"You and I have both done things we aren't proud of to protect the people in our lives, Park. It doesn't make us bad people. It makes us loyal. We're good at our jobs."

I smirk over at her. "People assumed you were just a stylist until this went down, Shan. I think you blew Amelia's mind when she saw you handling that gun. I have to admit that even in the middle of the situation, it was a turn-on."

"Leave it to you." She smiles. Tilting her head to the side, she sneaks in a kiss.

Reaching forward, I grab her chin between my thumb and forefinger. "Do you want to truly know what the man standing in front of you did? The one you allow to touch your body? I *shouldn't* be touching you after what I did."

She jerks her chin out of my hand. "You mean the man I love? Because he's the one standing in front of me, and you forget that I know you. There's nothing you do that's gratuitous. If you did it, then it needed to be done. I have no doubt about that. In everything, I trust you, Parker. You have to realize that by now."

Her unwavering faith is enough to bring me to my knees. I don't deserve it. "On three separate occasions, I had to put men down to keep Tristan safe. All of them bothered me, but one more than others."

Wrapping her arms around my waist, she holds on tightly. "Tell me about it. Let me take your burden."

I close my eyes, leaning onto her shoulder. "He was young, not much older than I was when I went into special forces. Probably around twenty-one or so. I found him sneaking around the outside of the tent, looking for a way in."

"What do you think he was trying to do?"

She's trying to make this easier on me, and I love her for that, but there isn't a way to explain what I did in a more palatable way. "I know what he was doing. There was a gun in his hands, and he was strapped for a showdown. For a few moments, I followed him. My gaze watched as he looked for a weak spot in the tent, but there wasn't one. I made sure of that when it was decided that's where Tristan would be. Everything about that tent was made to my specifications in order for me to protect Tristan and myself."

"Of course, if you weren't safe, then how could you make sure he was? No one would think badly of you for doing what you have to."

My throat tightens, and I swallow roughly. I'm not sure she's going to think this of me when I tell her exactly what I did. "He wasn't great at what he was supposed to be doing. Instead of covering all the sides, he left a whole one exposed. He turned his back to me, and when he did, I attacked. Not with a weapon, because it would've made too much noise."

"So what did you do?" she questions softly, running her fingers through my hair, cradling my head in her palm.

"Broke his neck. Didn't even think twice about it."

"Parker, that's what you've been trained to do." She lifts my head off her shoulder and forces my eyes to meet hers. "This doesn't make me look at you differently."

"It should." My throat tightens, the same with my chest. "I shouldn't be touching you or be here with you right now. I don't deserve it."

"Yes, you do. If I have to spend the rest of my life proving to you that I love you just the way you are, I will."

Those words bring tears to my eyes. "I care about you, Shan, and I'll never be able to express how much."

CHAPTER 33
SHANNON

The man lying beside me in bed is the epitome of every single dream I've ever had. When I was a little girl living in Crona, the man I wanted for mine was strong, loyal, and willing to die for the people he cared for. Until I moved to Haldonia, I'd never met anyone like this.

The first time I was introduced to Parker? I knew he was it.

He's sleeping beside me after confessing what he did. Some women would be scared and worried. I'm not. He's never given me reason to. No matter what he's done with his hands or what he warns me about himself, I'm not going to give him up. I knew what I was getting into when I agreed to be with him.

"I love you," I whisper as I stroke his face, pushing his hair from his forehead.

His eyes pop open. "I love you, too. Hearing you say it is the best gift I ever could've been given, Shan, but where does this leave us? I'm not sure I'll ever be able to trust myself again."

"What do you mean?"

"I was able to kill men with my bare hands. How can I trust that I won't fly off the handle with you one day?"

Rolling my lips together, I contemplate telling him why I left Crona. Half of it was because of what I saw at the castle, but there was also something else. "You've confessed to me, now I'm going to confess to you. I left Crona because I didn't like what was going on in the castle and with the royal family. That's neither here nor there at this point, but the main reason I left was because of my own family."

His jaw tics. "What are you saying, Shan?"

Sitting up, I run a hand through my hair. "I've lived in fear of men in my life. The first one I feared was my own father. The reason I worked with the royal family was because they wanted me to be integrated with him. After I started working at the castle, he didn't introduce me as his daughter anymore. Do you know what he did?"

"I can imagine." He glances up at me before reaching out to rub my thigh.

"He told everyone, 'This is your future princess of Crona. She's working at the castle now, but I just know the prince is going to fall in love with her.' He would tell anyone who would listen. Then, he would get frustrated when I would come home and had no news to tell him."

I stop for a second, trying to collect my thoughts.

"You don't have to finish if you don't want to." He rolls over and places a kiss on my bare leg. "Parents are assholes. They're meant to love us, but too many of them build their lives around us. Instead of being proud of their accomplishments and letting us live our own lives, they decide to abandon their individuality and make our lives theirs. I ran into this too, but I have a feeling it wasn't as bad as what you were dealing with."

For him to know exactly what I was dealing with, I have to be honest. That's never been a strong suit with me when it comes to what happened before I fled Crona. "The longer I worked at the castle, and I didn't have a ring on my finger or any indication that there might be interest in me, the more he was disappointed. At first it was passive-aggressive remarks. Then it escalated to where he would verbally abuse me. The last time he asked me why I hadn't been fucked by one of the Calders yet. I spat at him."

"And what did he do?" Parker grinds his back teeth together. "Did he touch you?"

Thinking back to that night, I'd rather forget it, but I know I have to be honest with him. If I'm not honest about this, then what else will he think I'm lying about? "Yes, he slapped me across the face, ripped my blouse, and told me it was my fault we were living in poverty. He had this grand idea that one of the members of the royal family would look at me, fall in love, and sweep me off my feet. He was counting on me being the person to bring us out of our situation, and he thought it would be because I'm pretty."

"You're beautiful." His voice is reverent as he reaches up, cupping my cheek in his calloused palm. "I don't think I ever told you what I thought when you walked into the room and my boss told me you were going to be Amelia's assistant."

Rising up on my knees, I face him. "No, you didn't, and I would love to hear that before I delve deeper into what I dealt with in Crona."

"At first, I didn't believe there was any way you'd be able to hold your own. You looked like you should've been the queen, or at the very least a princess. I went to my bosses and told them there was no way we'd be able to trust you with Amelia's wellbeing."

I cover my mouth with my hand and laugh loudly. "I guess I should be offended, but lots of people have underestimated me my entire life. It's part of what makes me good at my job. Everyone always assumes I'm a pretty face who doesn't know how to throw hands or handle a gun."

"Well, you know how to do both, and I've never been so turned on by a woman holding a gun before. I can tell you that." He leans up, kissing me roughly. "But keep telling me about your dickhead of a father."

I close my eyes, thinking about what was the last straw for my relationship with him. "I hated it, but I could deal with the things he was saying to me, until he started to give me tips on how to seduce older men. I didn't want that." I blink quickly to get the tears out of my eyes. "Then I went into work after watching what I was pretty sure was a sexual assault going down."

"Sexual assault? Shannon, no." He shakes his head as if he can't bear to hear what I'm about to say.

Crossing my arms over my knees, I go back to those moments when I was worried about what I was seeing. "I was never able to prove it, and after what I saw, I was scared to make accusations. But from that moment forward, I was always careful not to be alone with any of them."

"Why do I feel like there's a but coming?"

"Because there is."

His jaw tics as he holds it tight, but his gentle hands circle my thighs. "Tell me, I will kill the motherfucker. Whoever it is, I promise you, I will avenge you."

That's the sweetest thing anyone has ever said to me. "You don't have to do that."

"Oh, but I do. Tell me, Shannon."

"The King of Crona. He cornered me one night when I was working late. Since I suspected there was an assault, I'd made it a point not to be alone with any of the male members of the monarchy. That night, I knew I would be working later than normal, but I wasn't paying attention to who all was left in the wing of the castle I was in. When I was done with putting together some outfits for the queen, I checked to make sure I'd done everything I needed to." I stop for a second, swallowing to wet my now dry throat. "The shoes I wanted her to wear weren't there, so I left the room and didn't lock the door to the adjoining closet. I was bent over, looking for the box that held the ones I wanted."

"No, Shan..."

"It took me by surprise"—I take a deep breath, trying to hold back the shakes that are threatening to travel through my body—"when I felt a hand on my ass. Then there was one on the back of my neck, and I was being pressed further into the closet. It took me a few minutes to realize what was happening. The King of Crona was simulating doggy-style sex with me, while I was holding onto the carpet with my fingers for dear life." I'm ashamed as I tell the story to him. My cheeks are heated, and I keep trying to hide my face. But I have to continue telling him what happened. If I don't finish this now, I'm not sure I ever will be able to. "He stuck his hands up the back of my shirt and then pulled me back toward him. I was gagging because I could feel his length notching against my core. Although it was through clothes, it still felt violating."

"Because it was a violation. No one should ever do that to someone else. He assaulted you."

Tears fall from my eyes. "He one thousand percent did, but I felt as if it were my fault, because I didn't do anything when I saw what I believed was the first assault. For months, I let myself be shamed, and I made myself small." I do it again by trying to hide from him. "Then my father came at me with bullshit about how I was shaming the family because I hadn't been proposed to. I told him to fuck himself and left that night."

"Don't." Parker grabs hold of my chin. "Never try and hide yourself from me. There's no part of you that's going to make me think differently. The shit you've lived through? It's what makes you who you are, and it's what makes me love you."

My heart stutters in my chest. Every time he tells me he loves me, it's like the first time. "Parker, are you sure?"

He brings the back of my hand up to his lips. "I've never been more sure of anything in my life. I've been in love with you for a long time. It's never been easy for me to express my feelings and emotions, probably one of the reasons why I've done so well at my job. There was nothing to keep me from putting my body in front of Tristan's. There's something now."

I throw my arms around him, holding on tight. "Do you think you should resign?" I whisper. "I don't want that. I like working with you. You are one of the only people I'm willing to trust Amelia and Tristan's safety to. What are we going to do?"

"We're going to talk to Tristan and explain that having something important to me will make me a better protector. Now I understand why he wants to go home to his wife at the end of the night. I want to do that too."

I'm sure he isn't proposing to me, but hopefully this means we'll be moving in that direction some point. Instead of speaking, I launch myself at him, throw my arms around his neck, and hold on for dear life.

CHAPTER 34
TRISTAN

I've been at the weekend house for the last few days. All four of us have been, decompressing from what we've dealt with over the past few months. I've already spoken with Amelia about how much I appreciate her being there for me and the people of Haldonia. The ones I haven't spoken with are Shannon and Parker.

When I come downstairs, leaving Amelia upstairs under the covers, Shannon and Parker are kissing in the kitchen. "Sorry to interrupt." I smirk at the two of them.

They've been sure to keep their relationship private. If it wasn't for them sleeping in the same room, I would honestly have no idea they are together, as they don't do public displays of affection and hardly ever talk about one another.

"Your Majesty." Parker steps back, putting his hands behind him and gripping the countertop. "Is there something I can help you with?"

"I wouldn't say no to a cup of coffee."

Without asking, he turns around and starts making it. Besides Amelia, Parker is the person who knows me better than anyone else. "Do you want cream or not?" See, he knows me well enough to know that sometimes I like it, other times I don't.

"Yes, if you don't mind."

As I watch him make the coffee, I think about what I'm going to say to the two of them. They've done a lot to protect my family, and I want to give them a gift. "When I tell you this, I want you to keep an open mind. There isn't a precedent for any of this. Not what we just went through, not what you have been requested to do, and not what you've done. I looked it up in the history of Haldonia, and this has never been done."

"Tristan." Parker crosses his arms over his chest. "You don't have to do anything for me. The honor of my life has been taking care of you. Not only are you my king, but you're one of the best friends I ever had. I didn't anticipate that. When I was told that I was being assigned to your detail, I was so annoyed." He laughs. "Because I had this preconceived notion of who you were. Which was my fault, and I was quickly put in my place." He turns his gaze over to Shannon. "Then I saw her."

Chuckling, I nod. "Yeah, the first moment I saw the two of you together, I knew something was up. It took you a long time to admit it though."

"I have never admitted it, not to anyone except her." He tilts his head down toward her. "So you can assume you know what's going on, but I've never said it."

She rolls her eyes, throwing him a smirk. "He loves to be the one to say he's never admitted it. Hell, I'm lucky he's admitted how he feels about me. This man is a steel trap."

I'm surprised when I watch her reach over and wrap her arms around him. He opens his up and pulls her into him, dropping a kiss on her head. This is the first time I've seen the two of them offer any little bit of affection toward each other. Although I know they've been together for a while, I've never seen it before. "I was beginning to wonder if you were actually together or not. I could never catch you sneaking anything."

He smirks. "I was taught to keep my private life private. I became pretty good at it after a while."

He's never talked much about his time in special forces, so I'm interested to hear why he was told to do that. "What was the reason? You hardly ever share anything, so consider me all ears."

Parker walks around the island and pulls out one of the stools before dropping onto it. "You all might as well sit down. This could take a while."

Shannon and I share a look before we do as he's asked.

"Back in special forces, there was a big emphasis on keeping parts of our lives private. We were told not to have social media, and if we did to keep it scrubbed. To not allow anyone to know if there were people important to you. So almost none of the people who were serving with me had any of that." He runs a hand through his hair and then scratches at the couple-days-old beard on his jaw. "Our superiors were scared that if someone knew we had people important to us—kids, significant others, parents—they would use them to get to us."

Shannon nods, taking a drink of her coffee. "I can see that. If people know there's a way they can bribe you, they will. It's unfortunately very easy for the enemy to find out too many things about you with the simple click of a button. Once they have that information, they can use it to do what they wish. Which means they can try to get state secrets. It would be way too easy, and it's a matter of national security."

"Exactly. Which is why neither of us wanted anyone to know we were together." Parker grabs her hand, holding it so that we all can see it. "I was worried that someone would accuse us of things we weren't doing. Then there was a fear that someone would use her to get to me."

I choose my words carefully as I talk to the two of them. "The last few months have shown us a lot of things. It's been extremely eye-opening how quickly life can change. How things we thought would never be a worry, were. I can't tell you the last time I was truthfully worried that another country would invade Haldonia. To be honest, it was never."

They murmur their agreement, and I continue.

"Crona did a lot of things. Most of them god-awful. There are citizens of our country who will never be the same. I count myself as one of them." I take a drink from my coffee cup. "When I close my eyes, I still see shit from out there on the battlefield. Will that ever change? I'm not sure, and I'm not sure whether I want it to. Before we were invaded and forced to defend our position, I took everything for granted. It wasn't until we were stuck in the middle of that tent did I actually realize how different life was going to be."

I'm getting to my point, but it's important for me to explain to Parker and Shannon how much they mean to me, how they've become a part of our family through all the trials and tribulations we've had.

"So, what I've learned over the past few months is that life isn't promised, and we could lose it all within the blink of an eye. There's something I want to give the two of you. It's never been given to a security detail for the king in the past. But I want my monarchy to be different. I want to be the type of king who leads by example and making the changes instead of talking about them. Words only mean so much."

Parker's eyes meet mine. "I think I know what you're going to do."

He's a smart man. I have no idea he's probably thought of this before. "The changes I want to make are plentiful, but they start with the two of you. We couldn't have asked for better people to help protect us while we were going through this time. You all served your positions with great pride, which is why I want to offer you this."

"Tristan..." Parker turns to Shannon. "Is this what I think it is?"

Shannon is stumped. It's obvious in the way she keeps looking between the two of us.

"I'd love to be the king to give you the option to marry if that's what you want. To let you have a family if that's what you want. I know there are risks to it. Fully aware of that, but I'm willing to take those risks if you all are," I finish, knocking my knuckles against the granite. "Of course this is a decision you two will need to make, but I won't stand in your way if that's where you see your future going. Neither will Amelia. We will be happy to stand by your sides. To let our child grow up next to yours. It would be an honor."

She's quietly crying, and Parker appears to be barely keeping it together.

"Your Majesty, I don't know what to say." Parker's voice is quiet as if he can't believe what I've said.

"There's nothing to say. Just know I'm right behind you if this is what you want. All I ask is that you invite me to the wedding."

Shannon giggles. "I'd fully expect you to come off the nicest cathedral in the country for us. I mean, you can't offer this and then not let us go all out. I'm a stylist."

Parker slings his arm around her neck. "Who could kill with her bare hands. Damn, I don't think you know how hot that is."

Picking up my coffee, I take it to the bedroom, waiting for Amelia to wake up. As I look out at the ocean below us, I toast to myself. Here's to more quiet mornings with the people I care about, and the woman I love.

CHAPTER 35
AMELIA

This is the first time I've woken up in recent history that I'm not worried about where my husband is and if he's alive. It's amazing how much stress that takes away from my day to day. He might not be in bed next to me, but I don't have to worry he's freezing or bleeding out somewhere with no one who cares for him.

"Morning, Lia."

There he is. His strong, velvet-laced voice is what I dreamed of while he was gone. It's what I listened to in my dreams. To know he's here right now, and I don't have to listen to old videos on my phone is a relief. "Good morning, yourself."

When I lift my head off the pillow, I'm assaulted by the smell of coffee. It used to be one of my favorite scents, but it rolls my stomach. I clamp a hand over my mouth.

"Are you okay?" he asks, setting down the offending cup. He walks over to me before taking a seat on the bed. "You're awfully pale. Are you well?"

I don't know what to say. I'm nauseous and my gag reflex is working overtime. I haven't puked since I was a teenager. In fact, I do everything I can to prevent it because it's so awful. "Maybe it's the last few months? The stress I thought was over as soon as you came home, but maybe it affected me more than I imagined it would? I've noticed over the last few days, certain smells trigger it, and I'm exhausted. But that's to be expected since I didn't sleep well while you were gone."

He lays down on the bed and tucks me into his side. "I didn't either. I worried that someone would be trying to hurt you. There were so many days I just knew I'd get a message that you'd been taken, and they were holding you hostage to get to me. Literally my worst fear. It had me on edge every day."

"Me too," I answer back. Do I admit to him my worst fears too? Now that we've made it through, it seems that it would be the right thing to do.

"What are you thinking about so hard I can almost hear you."

I reach down, smoothing the blanket over me. "I've always been taught to look forward, not to focus on the past. The only way to continue to make changes within our lives is to put our heads down and keep pushing. But I'm having trouble with that, Tris. I'm not the same person I was a few months ago."

"Neither am I." I pull her hand to my chest, holding it over my heart. "We've both changed, and there's no way of going back to the people we were before. It doesn't mean we can't make who are now the people we've always wanted to be. There have been changes, but who's to say they aren't for the better? We've grown, and that's not a bad thing."

"But I'm more scared than I was before," I admit. "I used to look outside and want to walk in the grass, go for a ride on your bike, or go down to the fish and chips place. Now? Outside seems so scary. What if we go outside and someone is waiting there to make an example out of us? What if they're waiting for us to walk out and they want to end us? These are the things I worry about. Will I ever be the carefree person I was before? The one who could enjoy life?"

He pulls me tighter into his side. "It's going to take time, Lia. We can't go right back to the people we were before this. They don't exist anymore. Experiences and time have picked us up, molded us, and we've come out on the other side. I'm not saying we're better or worse, I'm just saying we're different."

There's a secret I've been keeping, and I'm not sure if now's the time to share it with him or not. But if the last few months have taught me anything, we can't wait for what's going to be the perfect time. If we hold off, we might lose it. "Tristan, I think I'm pregnant," I blurt out, my heart pounding against my chest. "I think that's why your coffee made me want to puke."

He opens his mouth, then closes it. Once. Twice. A third time. "Lia, are you sure? Is that why you've been tired lately?"

"I'm not sure because I haven't taken a test. I've been scared to. In the middle of all this uncertainty, I didn't want to stress you out by possibly bringing a baby into it. Not to mention we didn't know what the future looked like. Tris, it was so up in the air. None of us knew if Haldonia would even be a country. It was one of those things where if I put my head in the sand and ignored it, I was hoping by the time I needed to know, I could find out without anxiety."

He chuckles, reaching out and tipping my chin to him. "How's that going for you?"

"Not great," I admit, laughing along with him. "Obviously I'm going to have to know the answer sooner or later. It isn't as if this is going to go away."

"No, it's not going away. Why don't you take the test? I'm here now. You have one, I assume."

I do, and from everything I've heard, it's best to take in the morning, but now I'm scared. Both of it being positive and negative. On the one hand, I'm happy to have his child, on the other hand, what if I'm not pregnant and I've convinced myself I am. I'm going to be devastated, and after what we've been through, I'm not sure I can handle it. "Okay." I take a deep breath. "I'm not sure how I'm going to react when I find out. I don't want you to think I'm crazy."

"It's okay, Lia. None of us know how we're going to react in situations. I've learned that from what we've just gone through. We do the best we can, and we appreciate the emotions we have. I'll be happy either way, as long as you are."

I'm still not sure what I did to deserve this man. Although our marriage was arranged, I like to think I would've picked him if given a choice. He's everything I would've chosen. "Okay, I'll be right back."

Getting up out of bed, I put my feet on the floor, and the room spins slightly. Another indication that I might actually be pregnant. I don't say anything to him, but I clear my throat and get my bearings. Slowly, I get up and walk to the bathroom. I've kept a couple of boxes of pregnancy tests in here for when this moment comes. Holding up a finger, I give him a wink and shut the door.

My hands shake as I grab the box, turn it over, and read the instructions. Once. Twice. When I'm satisfied that I know them front to back, I open the package and do my business.

When I'm done, I wash my hands and then set it on the counter. Going back out to where Tristan is waiting, I have a seat next to him on the bed. He pulls me close, running his hand up and down my arm. As we wait, my stomach is shaky with nerves. My mind goes back to the night I met him, and how unsure I was of what we were embarking on. How I was worried that he wouldn't like me, how scary it was to offer myself to a man who had never met me before. "Were you scared the night we met?" I ask him out of the blue.

He grins. It's the boyish one that reminds me of the pictures of him as a child. "Yeah, I mean, you were beautiful, standing there in the light coming off the fire. That dress you were wearing, and the way your hair was shining. I thought you'd run away screaming because you were young, and I wasn't sure if you'd actually say yes."

"I wasn't aware I had a choice back then." I reach out, grabbing his hand with mine. Flipping it over, I trace hearts on his palm. "But I saw you, and you were so handsome. There was so much pain behind your eyes. There wasn't any way I was going to let you go. I knew my future was with you, even if I didn't exactly know what that meant. We're going to build an amazing life together, Tris. I have no doubt about it. I've always trusted you, and I'll continue to do so."

The timer he set when I came out goes off. "Should we go together?" he asks.

"Yeah, I'd like that."

With our fingers entwined, we head to the bathroom together. My stomach is queasy with what this means. It's excitement and fear all wrapped into one. We walk to the counter and lean over as one. Right there in black words—pregnant.

Tears steam down my face as I bury my head in his chest and hold on tight. The next generation of the monarchy is coming, and I can't wait to see what my husband looks like as a father.

But more than anything, I'm thankful he's here to experience this with me. If that bomb had gone off closer to him and Parker—I'd be a widow raising a baby alone.

EPILOGUE
TRISTAN

This is the first address I'm giving to the people of Haldonia since learning that Amelia and I are going to have a baby. I've been going back and forth about whether we should announce or if we should show up in public with a child after she has it. There are advantages to both situations. It's been three months since we found out, and it's officially okay for us to let people know.

Although we're picking up the pieces of war, it hasn't been easy. We've run into roadblocks here and there. Including a small almost-uprising in Haldonia.

"Our citizens need something good," Lia says as she looks over at me.

It's amazing how much her body has changed even in three months. The dress she's wearing is filled out at the top, and there's a slight swell at her stomach. Every time I see it I'm hit with the knowledge that it's my baby inside her. The two of us will be continuing the monarchy, and our line. Walking over to her, I place my hand on her stomach and lean in, giving her a kiss. "Well, we have something good, at least."

She rolls her eyes but accepts my kiss. "It's not going to be hidden very much longer, Tristan. It was easier as people were trying to get their lives back together and social media over here was getting back online. They didn't expect to see me all the time, so they didn't get a chance to notice how pale and sick I was during that first trimester. We've enjoyed this time together, but I think it's good that we share with the people. They need something to look forward to, too. While all of them won't be excited, a good number of them will. Maybe this is the chance to bring everyone together again, Tristan."

I hear what she's saying, but there's a part of me that's worried. If we make an announcement, it will be on the balcony of the castle, just like our marriage announcement was. That puts us right in the crosshairs of anyone who wants to do us harm. Coming back from where we just did, I'm concerned. We were attacked out of nowhere. "Are you sure? Shannon and Parker will be there with us, but I'm still worried. The invasion and attack have left me with scars that I don't know I'll ever be able to get rid of, Lia. You're the one thing that kept me sane through all of it, and I don't want to give anyone a reason to want to hurt you."

She reaches up, palming my cheek. "I understand your fear. I have it too. But this is a happy time. Let's share it with them. I think your mom would want that."

"All right. If that's what you wish, we'll tell them today."

"I do." She smiles that serene smile of a woman who knows she's going to be the best mother in the world.

"There are a few more things I need to talk about before I leave," I tell the crowd that's gathered below us. There's a round of applause, the same they've given us with every word I've said today.

She and I look at one another, and I give her a soft smile.

"As we look to the future for Haldonia, there are many things we're happy to be bringing. We're working on rebuilding, and while I realize we haven't gotten to every part of the city, we are working on it. Those of you who haven't seen the reconstruction crew, please fill out the government assistance forms, and we'll get you taken care of."

I take a moment and look out at the crowd, committing it to

memory. Reaching over, I pull Amelia to me and stand her in front of me. Wrapping my arms around her waist, I put my hands on her stomach. "The last announcement we have for today is that the future of Haldonia is here with us today. Your queen and I will be having the next generation of our family, and we hope you'll celebrate that miracle with us."

There are shouts and claps all around. Amelia turns into my arms, and we share a sweet kiss on the balcony.

Parker groans as he's been known to do. "You know that's going to be on the cover of all the magazines tomorrow."

It's become what I expect him to say with every public display of affection. Reaching over, I grip his shoulder. "Damn right, Park. One day it'll be you, but until then? My wife and I are going to turn the chaos into love."

Little did we know that would be harder than we ever thought imaginable.

A LOOK AT BOOK THREE
ROYAL LOVE

He's a king fighting battles no one can see. She's a queen torn between duty and love. Now, their love must withstand its greatest trial.

As Haldonia begins to rebuild, Tristan and Amelia should be embracing the promise of a new chapter. But as they prepare for the arrival of their first child, Tristan finds himself trapped in a war of his own. Determined to be the strong, unshakable ruler his people need, he hides his pain behind duty—unaware that with every step he takes to protect Amelia, he's pushing her further away.

Amelia has spent her life preparing to be queen, but nothing could prepare her for watching the man she loves slip through her fingers. Seeking comfort in her growing bond with the people of Haldonia, she throws herself into her role, even as the distance between her and Tristan deepens. But when his struggles threaten to consume him, Amelia is forced to make an impossible choice: stand by and let him face his demons alone, or risk everything to bring him back to her.

With their marriage hanging by a thread and the future of their family in jeopardy, Tristan and Amelia stand at a crossroads—fight for each other or watch everything they've built fall apart. Love once made them unstoppable, but can it mend what's breaking, or will the fractures between them become too deep to heal?

AVAILABLE JULY 2025

Laramie Briscoe is the *USA Today* and *Wall Street Journal* bestselling author of over thirty books, with sales of over half a million copies.

Since self-publishing her first book in May of 2013, Laramie has appeared on the Top 100 Bestselling E-books Lists on Amazon Kindle, Apple Books, Barnes & Noble, and Kobo. Her books have been known to make readers laugh and cry. They are guaranteed to be emotional, steamy reads.

When she's not writing alpha males who seriously love their women, she loves spending time with friends, reading, and marathoning shows on Netflix. Married to her high school sweetheart, Laramie lives in Bowling Green, Kentucky, with her husband (the Travel Coordinator) and an adorable dog named Gus.

www.laramiebriscoe.net

www.ingramcontent.com/pod-product-compliance
Lightning Source LLC
Chambersburg PA
CBHW010838250626
47157CB00011B/3309